Of Sound Mind

JEAN FERRIS

Of Sound Mind

FARRAR STRAUS GIROUX

NEW YORK

Copyright © 2001 by Jean Ferris

All rights reserved

Distributed in Canada by Douglas & McIntyre Ltd.

Printed in the United States of America

Designed by Filomena Tuosto

First edition, 2001

1   3   5   7   9   10   8   6   4   2

Library of Congress Cataloging-in-Publication Data

Ferris, Jean, date.

Of sound mind / by Jean Ferris.— 1st ed.

p. cm.

Summary: Tired of interpreting for his deaf family and resentful of their reliance on him, high school senior Theo finds support and understanding from Ivy, a new student who also has a deaf parent.

ISBN 0-374-35580-0

[1. Children of deaf parents—Fiction.   2. Deaf—Fiction.   3. Physically handicapped—Fiction.   4. American sign language—Fiction.   5. Family problems—Fiction.   6. Friendship—Fiction.]   I. Title.

PZ7.F4174 Of 2001

[Fic]—dc21

00-68123

I exist as I am, that is enough.

—Walt Whitman, *Song of Myself*

Although the grammar and syntax of American Sign Language are quite different from those of English, for purposes of clarity I have transliterated the conversations in ASL into standard English.

The signed conversations are printed in a different font from the rest of the text so that it's clear when words are being spoken and when they're being signed.

In contrast to the usual convention of using "deaf" to refer only to the physical condition of deafness and "Deaf" to refer to identification with the full Deaf culture, I have chosen to use "deaf" exclusively to avoid confusion and distraction in what is a fictional narrative, not a factual discussion of the complexities of deafness.

Of Sound Mind

1

Theo watched the bus filling up, knowing he should get on now if he wanted a seat. But he didn't move. If he got on this bus, he'd be home in twenty-five minutes. If he missed it and waited for the next one, he'd be home in forty-five minutes.

Forty-five sounded better.

He noticed that he had begun to mutter with his hands, an impulse that came automatically to those, like him, who had learned American Sign Language as a first language. For all of his preschool years, he'd spoken more in sign than in English, and there were times, even now, when he forgot, as he'd done then, that it wasn't always necessary.

He quieted his hands as he noticed a girl with shining, chin-length dark hair watching him as she waited to board the bus. He thought he'd seen her around school, but with over a thousand students to sort through in the second week of his senior year, he wasn't sure. She flicked a final glance in his direction and got on.

When she turned her back on him, he knew he'd never seen her before. He would have remembered the single strand of hair, dyed purple and threaded through with colorful beads that reached below her shoulder blades.

The doors closed behind her, and the bus pulled away in a blast of diesel fumes. Her dark eyes watched him from the window in a way that made it hard for him to look at anything else.

Wow, he signed unconsciously, **who is she**? and forced his thoughts to turn toward home again.

So what if his mother had to wait twenty more minutes for him to make her phone calls for her. So what if Jeremy had to wait twenty more minutes to have help with his fifth-grade homework. No matter how much help he had, nobody at his school expected much from a deaf kid, even in his special classes.

Immediately, Theo felt guilty. Jeremy tried so hard. The only reason he bugged Theo so much about help with his homework was because he wanted to be a regular kid, not a freak or a failure. It was different with Palma. For her, Theo was a tool, an instrument, an extension of her will— at least, that's how he saw it.

He leaned back against the bus bench and let the late August afternoon sunlight slant onto him. He closed his eyes and took a fifteen-minute vacation, going off someplace where he got to do whatever he wanted, whenever he wanted. Fantasies were good. They were sanity-saving, even if they had no chance of ever becoming reality, and he used them freely.

The next bus was a few minutes late, so Theo had a longer mental vacation than he'd counted on. But as soon as he got through the front door at home, it was over. Both Jeremy and Palma were on him, signing at him hard and fast.

Stop, he signed back. **I can't watch you both at the same time.**

Palma leaned over Jeremy's shoulders and took his hands in hers, folded them across his chest, and patted them firmly, shutting him up as surely as if she'd put her hand over a speaker's mouth. It was about the rudest thing one signer could do to another, not that Palma would care about something like that. Jeremy pushed her hands away, but he knew better than to start signing again.

Theo, you know I have to make sure my show is organized. Palma's hands were going so fast he had trouble following them. **I need you to make calls for me.**

I made plenty of calls for you yesterday. What did Palma care that it was Sunday? She wanted her answers when she thought of her questions. **Besides, I thought you were doing most of it by e-mail**, he responded, even though he knew she couldn't do it all that way, especially since she was so self-conscious about mistakes she might make when writing in English.

5

I can't do everything like that. You have to help me. Her hand smacked into her chest in the sign for *me*.

Me, Theo thought. That's who always comes first, isn't it? **Okay, okay. Who do you want me to call first?** What was the point of resisting or refusing? She always got her way. No wheel squeaked louder than she did, even though she rarely made an actual sound.

The gallery. They don't answer their e-mail. I need to know everything got there all right. I need to know the l-u-c-i-t-e—she finger-spelled the word—**pedestals are the right height.**

Theo made the call. Naturally the sculptures, all of them, had arrived safely. Palma had Theo make the gallery owner measure the pedestals twice. Both measurements were exactly the same, but Palma still doubted them.

Tell him if they're wrong, I'll shove one of those pedestals up his ass.

"My mother says thanks for all your help," Theo said into the phone. "She knows you understand how anxious artists can get about their work just before a show."

Theo never felt guilty about fudging his interpretations for her. If he'd correctly interpreted everything Palma had ever told him to, she'd have almost everybody she'd ever worked with out gunning for her. Of course, a licensed interpreter would get fired for that, but he gave himself more leeway than the pros got. Besides, he took some of the credit for how charming people thought his mother was.

Part of that impression was given by the way he edited what she said.

As soon as Theo hung up the phone, Palma signed, **Call him back. I want him to measure those pedestals again. I don't trust him as far as I can throw him.**

Obediently, Theo picked up the phone and began to punch in the numbers. But he held the phone so that Palma couldn't see he had pressed down the button that would make a real call possible. He carried on an animated conversation with absolutely nobody while his mother kept giving him more messages about what she wanted him to say.

Then he called the dressmaker to make sure Palma's dress would be ready in plenty of time, fitting perfectly; the airlines to reconfirm, for the fourth time, that her tickets were okay; the hotel, to make sure, for the third time, that her room would have a teletypewriter—a TTY—so she could call home and nag from a distance until the rest of the family arrived for her show's opening. There were other calls, too, while Jeremy waited, shifting from one foot to the other, eager for Theo's attention but afraid to annoy Palma again.

After he'd made the last call, Palma threw her arms around Theo and hugged him lavishly, smiling her gorgeous smile, then backed off, signing, **You are wonderful. The biggest help in the world. How would I ever get along without you?** She whirled in a circle, pulling Jeremy around with her by the same hands she'd previously used to silence him. She dropped his hands and signed, **I'm going to the studio**. In a gust of perfume and flying skirts, she left the room.

Once again Theo was aware of how complicated communicating by sign was. Palma couldn't do it while she hugged him. She couldn't do it while she held Jeremy's hands. Neither could Jeremy. She couldn't do it if nobody would look at her, or if it was dark, or if her arms were full. Those were things he supposed she and Jeremy and his father were all used to and accepted without thinking, since they'd been deaf all or most of their lives and never communicated any other way—except for paper and pencil, which required the same monopoly on hands. But Theo, who was bilingual, easily saw the advantages and disadvantages of both languages, sign and English.

Having two languages was supposed to be an advantage. He knew that. But what it felt like to him was a suspension, leaving him hanging between two lives. He wasn't deaf, but he didn't seem fully hearing either. He was like one of those charioteers in ancient Rome trying to ride with each foot on a separate horse. It was possible, but just barely, and it was really uncomfortable. Either horse would have been better than both.

Without his realizing it until he'd already done it, his hands had made the signs for several bad words.

Jeremy laughed, the slightly unearthly sounds of someone who'd never heard his own voice, and signed, **You said something bad. Are you mad at Palma?**

Theo took a deep breath and decided, for Jeremy's sake, that he should act like a sensible older brother—not like the surly adolescent he was at the moment.

Everybody gets mad at their family sometimes, Jeremy. It's normal. And it goes away.

Okay, Jeremy signed. **I was pretty mad at her, too. For grabbing my hands. I hate it when she does that.**

I know. She used to do that to me, too.

But she doesn't anymore?

No. I made her stop.

How?

I told her I wouldn't interpret for her anymore if she didn't cut it out.

But I can't do that. Jeremy looked thwarted at the prospect of finding a sufficient threat to stop Palma. **Pop never does stuff like that. He lets you talk even if he doesn't like what you're saying.**

Pop's different from Palma, that's all, Theo signed. **He's not as** . . . as what? High-strung? Demanding? Selfish? **Impatient,** was the word he finally signed. He'd allow Jeremy the privilege of figuring Palma out for himself.

When's she going to Boston? Jeremy asked.

Day after tomorrow.

And when do we go?

Friday. That's when her show opens. We'll be there

for the weekend and we'll all come home together.
Unless she changes her mind, the way she usually does,
Theo thought, and wants to stay around being fawned over
and watching people admire her work. Not that he ever
minded when she extended her trips.

**Okay now, let's see what's going on with your
homework.**

The next day was even worse. Palma was in a frenzy of
packing, and arranging, and leaving instructions about
things she'd already told them a hundred times, snapping
and sniping and driving herself to tears. No matter how
many times Theo had seen her behave like that, and knew
it was just nerves over her show, he still wished she were
going off to a convent in Tibet. A hotel in Boston wasn't
nearly far enough from their house in Philadelphia.

Jeremy stayed in his room, lying low and hiding out until the next morning, when she'd be gone and they'd have a
couple of days of peace and male camaraderie with their
father, who, by this point, Theo was regarding as either a
saint or a fool for getting involved with Palma to start with.

Theo knew the story of their courtship, but still didn't
really get what had brought them together. Maybe it
was just the fact that deaf people mostly married other
deaf people, which gave them a smaller pool of potential
spouses to choose from.

They'd met in college, at Gallaudet, the school Palma

considered it her sovereign right to attend since she was the offspring of two deaf parents and three deaf grandparents, all of whom had gone to Gallaudet. Never mind that it was the only four-year liberal arts college in the world for deaf people, and that every deaf person alive had probably at least thought of going there, even if they never actually applied, and that the competition to get in was fierce. Palma never doubted for an instant she'd be admitted.

Theo's father, Thomas, on the other hand, had been deafened at eight by meningitis and was the only deaf kid in any school he ever went to before he got to Gallaudet. He'd told Theo once that when he was first deafened, he didn't think he'd live to be an adult because he'd never seen a grown-up deaf man. He figured somehow they all died early from their deafness. Thomas's parents, whom Theo never knew, were good-hearted, but didn't know how to get him the help he needed, and never learned to sign very well except for the made-up signs—home sign—they used around the house. Because Thomas could speak and read before he got meningitis, no one quite believed he was as deaf as he actually was, which caused all kinds of misunderstandings: teachers thought he was deliberately inattentive, his mother thought he was obstinate, his father thought he was disrespectful, and his classmates teased him. So when he got to Gallaudet—which he'd never even known about until he was seventeen—mostly through the pull and push from his high school guidance counselor, he was ecstatic. He thought he'd been transported to heaven, and he never got over being amazed at his lucky break, and grateful.

He'd taught himself to sign from a book the summer before college, but what he knew was nothing like the real stuff: what he was doing was like trying to speak Latin in modern Italy. But once he was there, he caught on fast, and every day was a picnic to him. Between his great good humor, his ability to perform apparently impossible magic tricks, and his outstanding athletic abilities, he was wildly popular.

It probably made sense that Palma, the golden girl, the beauty, the one everybody wanted to please just to see her smile, would feel that the school's most popular guy was hers for the taking. The way Palma told it, she could have had any guy at Gallaudet—or anywhere else—that she'd wanted, but she'd picked Thomas because his long eyelashes were so cute. If this was true, there was clearly much Theo didn't understand about the laws of attraction. Thomas must have been plain dazzled by her, the way almost everybody was, at least at first, and wowed by his good fortune. And he'd never gotten over it; the fact that she'd become famous while he remained a furniture-maker only made him more nuts about her. Thomas was a guy who thought the most ordinary day was as good as a birthday present. He knew how to *carpe diem*, no doubt about it.

2

Wednesday after school, Theo rushed to be on one of the first buses. Palma had left that morning, Jeremy was going to a friend's after school, and Theo could have the house to himself for the afternoon with no chores, no phone calls, no hassles. He'd turn the music up and not feel guilty about being the only one who could enjoy it; he could work out with his weights and shoot some hoops with the guys across the street and surf the Web without interruptions. Then the Posse, as Thomas called the three of them when Palma was away, would have pizza and root beer floats and hot fudge sundaes, a totally satisfying meal that Palma would have regarded as nutritional suicide (never mind her own irregular eating habits), and watch a movie rented from the Deaf Services Library that had subtitles but didn't even need them because it would be almost all action.

Palma didn't like the subtitled movies. She preferred to

watch without aids that interfered with her making up her own plots to the visuals. Just like her, Theo always thought, to want to be the one in charge.

He smiled in anticipation and found his smile going right into the furious face of the girl with the purple hair on the other side of the window just as the bus pulled away without her. He looked back at her in time to see her, to his amazement, saying several pretty bad words in sign language.

What was he, some kind of magnet for deaf people? Without trying, did he draw them to him? Even in a school of more than a thousand, he and she were probably the only two signers, unless she had an interpreter who went to class with her. But there was no way he was going to let her in on the fact that he knew her language. He already had enough people he had to interpret the world for.

He just wished he hadn't taken that first zowie look at her two days before.

Thomas brought home the Mega-Pizza as well as Jeremy, whom he'd picked up on the way.

The cavalry is here, he signed as Theo came out of his room, rubbing his eyes from too much time staring at the computer screen. He'd finished the homework for his advanced calculus class as well as done all the extra credit work, and still had had time for some computer games, even after doing his full routine on the weights. The guys across the street had said basketball tomorrow—no time today. That was fine with Theo. Tomorrow would be another day without Palma.

Charge, Jeremy signed, running the pizza to the kitchen and plonking it on the table Thomas had made before either of them were born—a sturdy round of oak on a pedestal with playful bear paws for feet. Palma wasn't so sure about the paws, but Jeremy and Theo loved them.

During their dietary disaster, they all tried to sign at once, talking at the same time, teasing, joking in a way they never did when Palma was there presiding over lettuce leaves and baby vegetables at the glass-and-steel dining room table.

I want to get a tattoo, Jeremy signed.

Okay. Thomas took another piece of pizza.

Okay? Jeremy's eyes were wide with disbelief. **Just like that?**

Sure. Thomas chewed. **You can get anything you like: tiger, eagle, Harley-Davidson.**

Darth Vader?

Darth Vader, no problem. As long as you get it on your face.

My face? But I want it on my arm. That's where it'll look cool. That's where everybody gets them.

Thomas gave him a serious look. **Jeremy, you are a unique, special, one-of-a-kind model. Why would you want to be like everybody else? Let *them* want to** look like **you**. He took a swig of his root beer float. **Tell you what. If you want somebody else to have one on his face, I'll get one, too. Maybe Theo will, too. We'd really be the Posse then. Maybe we'd even start a trend. How about it, Theo?**

Sounds good to me. I've always wanted a Tweety Pie on my forehead.

Never mind. Jeremy could give a sulky intonation even in sign. He dropped his hands into his lap, where they muttered insulting words about the rest of the Posse.

Theo had to force himself not to smile. He wished Jeremy's cussing didn't remind him so much of the way the purple-haired girl had signed to herself outside the bus that afternoon.

The bright light connected to the telephone blinked, indicating a phone call. Thomas answered and was greeted with a rapidly filling screen, messages from Palma checking up on them.

We had pork chops and baked potatoes for dinner, Thomas typed in return. *The boys'll do the dishes while I start the laundry. Then we're going to get tattoos.*

What? Palma typed.

Just a joke, Peach-pot. We're really going to get our tongues pierced. Why should you be having all the fun?

If you think this is fun, you're crazy. They had everything wrong. I've been working like a coal miner all day.

Theo was sure the gallery had done everything just

16

the way Palma wanted. The only thing wrong was, she'd changed her mind.

My poor darling, Thomas typed.

The screen was quiet, waiting.

Theo could just imagine Palma deciding whether to stay up there on her high horse or to recognize Thomas's good-will in spite of her irritation at being played with.

Well, I'm glad you're doing all right without me, she replied neutrally.

Only barely existing without our Princess, Thomas typed, and winked at the boys.

I'll bet you had pizza for supper and you really are going to get tattoos. You probably already have them.

Thomas opened his eyes wide and waved his arms in comic panic before typing, *We can't hide our crimes from you, my love. I hope you like the Tweety Pie Theo has on his forehead.*

HA HA. See you Friday. Love, Palma.

Then they each typed their names: *Thomas. Theo. Jeremy.* And hung up.

Might as well get the tattoos now, Jeremy, Thomas signed. **She's expecting them.**

Later, as they watched the video, Jeremy leaned against Thomas's side with his father's arm slung casually around his shoulders. Absently, Jeremy played with Thomas's fingers, callused from his work. Theo watched the two of them, thinking Jeremy might as well have been playing with his father's heart. His hands were his lifeline: the way he communicated, made his living, expressed his humor and his creativity, showed his love. If Theo had to depend on just his hands to do all that, he'd be afraid to ever take them out of his pockets.

3

At school the next day, Theo found himself looking for that hank of purple hair, the colorful beads, the big dark eyes. He didn't want to be doing that, but his mind was out of his control, maybe taken over by the same aliens who had made him the only hearing member in an all-deaf family.

After looking for her between every class period with no success, he was startled to find himself unexpectedly right next to her at the end of the school day when it seemed as if the whole school was trying to squeeze through the exit doors at the same time. She hitched her backpack higher on her shoulder and signed, **Hi**.

The crush of students pushed him through the doors ahead of her while he ransacked his mind: should he pretend he didn't know what she was doing? Then that would be the end of . . . well, of nothing, actually. Or should he sign back? Then he'd be in it for sure: friend to the friendless, interpreter of the world, caught forever whether he liked it or not because a decent guy never deserted somebody who needed him, no matter how much he might want to.

Out on the steps in the cool of the early fall afternoon, she was beside him again. **Hey. Don't be shy. I saw you signing to yourself the other day at the bus stop. I didn't know there was anybody else around here who knew ASL. What a surprise.**

Was she assuming he was deaf, too? Newly mainstreamed like her? **Hi**, he signed guardedly.

Are you new here too?

Three years. He was trying to be quick and inconspicuous, reluctant to attract the stares he often got when he signed in public.

We just moved to Philadelphia. She paused, looking up at him with her big dark eyes. **How do you like it?**

It's okay.

Were you at a deaf school before? she asked.

He hesitated. **Actually** . . . He hesitated again. **Actually, I'm not deaf. My parents are. And my brother. That's why I can sign.**

"Oh." She spoke, her eyebrows lifted. "Silly me. I made an assumption. My father says that's almost always a mistake, and now I know he's right."

"Hey." His voice was breathy with surprise. "You mean you're hearing, too?"

She was shoved against him by a rush of students hurrying to get on the first bus. "Hey, Theo," one of the guys in the group called. "I'll see you as soon as I get home, man. First, basketball. Then that calculus assignment. It needs your expert explanation." He sped on, while Theo nodded an okay to him.

The top of the girl's head came to just beneath Theo's chin. Her hair smelled like summer, and she felt soft against him.

"Sorry," she said, separating herself from him. "Sorry, sorry, sorry." She laughed. "I was thinking maybe you were a confused new person who could stand a friendly word. I guess I forgot *I'm* the confused new person. And I didn't mean to get *that* friendly."

"It's okay. No problem." Absolutely no problem at all.

They stood in a pack of other kids at the bus stop, waiting for the next bus to come along.

"How come you know sign?" Theo asked. She had the greatest eyes, so dark and big, mild and sharp-looking at the same time. He was trying not to measure the length of her eyelashes, which were, according to Palma, the vital key to a relationship.

"Oh." She smiled, and a dimple big enough to hide a peanut in appeared. "My dad's deaf. My mother wasn't, but she doesn't live with us anymore. Besides, she never learned to sign as well as I can, so I did most of the interpreting, even when she was around."

"How did they manage to get married if she didn't sign very well?" he asked. The way he saw it, communicating was hard enough between two people who were fluent in the same language.

"Well." She gave him a sidelong look. "I was born six months after they were married. That may have had something to do with it."

Theo could feel the color rising in his face. God, what an idiot he was. What was he thinking, asking such a stupid, personal question?

She noticed, shrugged, and said, "Don't worry about it. It doesn't bother me. My dad was dying to have kids. He was thrilled. My mom—well, not so much, I guess. He says she stayed longer than he expected she would—I was nine when she left—and I'd rather be with my dad anyway. So it worked out okay for all of us. Ninety percent of marriages between a hearing person and a deaf person fail, you know."

"No," he said. "No, I didn't know that." But he wasn't surprised at the news.

The bus swooped up to the bus stop with a screech of brakes and that embarrassing farting sound stopping buses make.

"Is this your bus?" Theo asked, though he knew it was.

"Yes. Yours, too?"

He nodded and let her board ahead of him. While he was still worrying whether it would be presumptuous of him to sit next to her, she'd slid over on the seat and was looking expectantly up at him.

"We moved here at the beginning of the summer," she said, when he was seated. "My dad's this big computer guy and he got recruited or head-hunted or whatever from his last job to run a big project at Penn. More money, better opportunity, so he couldn't say no."

"Where did you live before?"

"Seattle. You ever been there?"

"Yeah, I have." They'd gone last year for one of Palma's shows. It was in the summer and they'd stayed a week. It rained the whole time, which everybody said it wasn't supposed to do in July, but they still had a great time. They sailed, went to movies and bookstores, and drank fancy coffee, and in the mild and misty summer days—such a contrast with the muggy, buggy fever heat of July in Philadelphia—it seemed as if they were doing it in an alternate universe. "I liked it. Lots to do."

"That's true. But the weather can get you down. And my shoes in the back of the closet always had mildew on them."

He sat silently, at a loss for how to respond to a remark like that, way too conscious of how close their hips were on the seat, how warm her arm was pressing against his. How relieved he was that she wasn't deaf.

He knew a few other hearing kids of deaf parents, ones he'd met at the Deaf Club Thomas liked to go to. Their slogan was "I don't know you, but I know you." Yet even with that bedrock recognition, he hadn't met anybody he gave a single thought to in between his rare visits to the club with Thomas. But friendships depended on more than having deaf parents in common. With this girl whose name was still a mystery, the attraction was there. He didn't know her, but he knew her. Maybe it was like discovering you were members of the same rare religious sect, or had the same unusual disease.

"Does your father ever go to Deaf Club meetings?" he asked her.

"No." She turned to face him. It was a habit signers had, watching others intently, alert to every facial alteration, every change of body position, all of which carried meaning. Looking away was seen as rude and uninterested, while unbroken eye contact, regarded as ill mannered and even insolent by hearing people, was considered courteous. For Theo it took conscious effort not to stare when talking to other hearing people.

"What are they like?"

He shrugged. "Lots of deaf people signing. A few hearing kids of deaf people signing." When she laughed, he felt guilty at having made even such mild sport of something so important, so pleasurable, to his father.

"My dad can speak to a lot of people through the computer or with his message service pager. Even his colleagues at work communicate with him that way. By the time he gets home in the evening, socializing is the last thing he wants to do. Usually he just wants to build his model airplanes."

"He builds models, too?"

"What do you mean, *too*? It's his only hobby."

"I just meant, a lot of deaf people have hobbies they do with their hands. They're so good with them. And those hobbies usually don't require a lot of talking. My dad does magic."

"Really? I never thought about that. I don't know much about deaf people. My dad's always been pretty buried in his work and his models. When my mom was still around, he spent time with her, but he says they didn't socialize much. I'm guessing maybe she was embarrassed about him—that somebody who looked like him could be so—so . . . well, what she apparently considered to be limited."

What did that mean, who looked like him? Theo wondered.

"Oh," she said, figuring out his puzzlement. "My dad is a very handsome man. He was on this calendar in Seattle— Ph.D. Hunks, or Dr. Hunks, or something like that. And he's forever got women trying to talk to him or making up some excuse for handing him their phone numbers. It's sort of fun to watch them discover he can't hear. Most of them act like they've found a worm in an apple." She looked out the window. "I get off here."

He stood to let her out.

She gave him a long look through her thick eyelashes. "Your name's Theo?"

"Yeah. How did you know?" He sounded stupid even to himself.

"I heard that guy on the steps outside school call you that. Nice to meet you, Theo."

"Likewise." She was already starting down the aisle before he remembered to ask, "What's your name?"

She turned back and smiled at him in a way that made her dimple show and his stomach get jittery. "Ivy Roper. Like Theo, it's easy to lip-read. Bye."

He sat down again with a thump. Ivy. Old-fashioned yet hip, in a folk-singer kind of way. A vine that could twine around you. He stopped that thought before his stomach got any more agitated.

4

He looked for her the next day, Friday, the day he was leaving for Boston. He wanted to tell her—well, he wasn't sure what he wanted to tell her: maybe that he'd like to see her outside of school, go to a movie or something; that he wanted to touch the beads in her purple hair; that he was still astonished that they had in common, of all unexpected things, deaf parents; that her signing was elegant and fluid, like a good magic trick itself. He just wanted to be able to talk to her again even though he knew he'd never actually say any of the things he'd been thinking about. He'd probably be too bulldozed to say anything at all.

He was saved from finding out how tongue-tied he'd be because he never saw her. Was she sick? Was she avoiding him? Did she have to go with her father to act as interpreter at the doctor's? The lawyer's?

He'd had to do that, more times than he could count. Of course, there were professional interpreters who could help, but they weren't plentiful, they had to be booked in advance, which meant planning ahead, something Palma wasn't good at, and they cost money. Why bother with all that when you had your own live-in one who was at your constant disposal, and who was, best of all, free?

He'd had to manage the purchase of their present home, with the lackadaisical help of their Realtor, negotiating with the seller, arranging the bank loan, and negotiating with the buyer of their previous house, when he was just eleven and didn't know what a lot of terms he had to use even meant, much less how to sign them to his parents. And the reason they were buying a new house was because Palma had suddenly been discovered by the art world and was selling her sculptures for such insane prices. Insane enough to easily pay for an interpreter for as much time as necessary. But no. According to Palma, Theo was the one for the job even if it meant keeping him out of school for as many days as she needed him.

Eleven, for Pete's sake. She'd let him buy a house then, but not pick out his own sneakers.

Thomas, on the other hand, hated to ask Theo for help, put it off as long as he could, used his ingenuity to do as much for himself as he could. But, no matter how he tried, he couldn't do everything without help. And, naturally, because Thomas hated to ask, Theo didn't mind helping him.

In fact, it made him angry to discover that Thomas, not wanting to impose, had been to the doctor by himself, struggling with lip-reading and pencil and paper and still not being certain he'd understood everything.

Why didn't you ask me, Pop? I'd have gone with you.

The only appointment I could get was at ten. I didn't want you to miss calculus. I know you love it.

Palma wouldn't know that. She wouldn't even know that Theo *took* calculus, never mind what time and how much he liked it.

But you need to know everything the doctor said. It's important.

It was just my annual physical. I'm healthy as a horse. He said I needed my crankcase drained and my spark plugs changed and my tires rotated. That's all.

So Theo had called the doctor himself and discovered that Thomas's cholesterol was high enough to require medication, and so was his blood pressure. That sounded pretty serious to Theo, though the doctor said not to worry, that both could be controlled if Thomas was careful and conscientious about his pills.

Hey, Pop, are you taking your medicine? The stuff the doctor wants you to take?

I don't feel bad. Why should I take something I don't need?

But you *do* need it. You're supposed to be taking it every day.

Thomas made a face. **Just another way for doctors to get rich. That stuff's expensive.**

Pop. You have medical insurance. That's what you pay premiums for. Will you promise you'll go get the medicine and take it?

Thomas stuck his thumbs in his ears and waggled his big callused hands at Theo. Then he signed, **You going to make me?**

Theo nodded. **Don't think I can't. Want to arm-wrestle?**

Thomas sat himself down at the kitchen table and plonked his elbow with his arm straight up, his hand open in invitation.

Theo held out for about thirty seconds and then it was all over. Thomas, who had kept up his college athletic habits, had arms like tree trunks, as strong and as rough.

Okay, you win, Theo signed. **Now will you take your medicine?**

If you want me to.

I do.

Once he'd beat Theo at arm wrestling, Thomas pulled a quarter from behind Theo's ear, made it disappear down the front of his shirt, and then plucked it again from his elbow.

You can't beat me at arm wrestling when you're all weighed down with change, Thomas said.

I wish I was. See how much more you can squeeze out of me.

Thomas gave him a good-natured rap on the head and signed, **I've got to go to the drugstore.**

Suspicion of hearing people—or "hearies," as Jeremy called them—by deaf people was widespread, and Thomas, who was so solid and sensible in most other ways, was not immune. Perhaps he'd been infected by Palma, whose paranoia and wariness could reach epic proportions, especially during the countdown to a show, when she thought everyone she had to deal with—and they were almost exclusively hearies—was somehow trying to sabotage her. So Theo wasn't entirely surprised that Thomas would question the doctor's diagnosis. But with something as important as his health, Theo thought he should be more trusting. He had to remember that, at the same time some deaf people thought hearies knew more than they did, they also thought hearies were always ready to con them, or play tricks on them, or make them look foolish.

Once, when he was about six, Theo had asked his father if the way the people at the Deaf Club felt about hearies extended to him. Thomas had looked astonished. **Of course not. You're not like that. You're not hearing, you're not deaf, you're just Theo.**

When he'd asked his mother, Palma had said, **Don't be**

ridiculous, and dismissed his concern with a flip of her eloquent hand.

Theo wanted to see Ivy to tell her he was going to Boston. He wanted to tell her about his father's health and his mother's art and Jeremy; about his dreams, and how beautiful a mathematical equation could be, and the satisfaction he got from the perfect three-pointer. And he wondered if she'd think he was nuts if he did that. Why should she care? Just because she had a deaf father, too, didn't mean she had to like him. She was new at their school and she was lonely and she'd seen him signing, that was all. The way she looked, she'd have ten new friends by Monday. She didn't need one as loaded as he was with conflict and resentment and guilt.

He hurried out to the buses, dodging his way between people, taking the stairs two at a time. He knew he should get the first bus—after all, he had a plane to catch and he had to get home fast. But he wanted to ride home with Ivy. Ivy, who wasn't at the bus stop. He waited through two buses until he couldn't wait any longer. He boarded and sat by the window, still craning for her. Where was she?

Just as the bus pulled away, he saw her come running for it, late and disheveled, accompanied by Claire Cassidy, one of the cheerleaders. Claire and Ivy looked at the bus pulling away, and then laughed, sagging against each other, breathless.

Theo twisted in his seat, watching them as they grew indistinct behind the lumbering bus. What was so funny? How had she and Claire, practically the most popular girl in school, gotten to be such buddies already? If she was going to be in that crowd, he'd never be able to even get close to her again. His dubious status as a math prodigy didn't carry much weight with Claire Cassidy's bunch.

He slumped back in his seat, his mood black. And ahead of him was a weekend with Palma, sure to be at her prima donna best.

The taxi was waiting at the front door when he came running down the street from the bus stop, with Thomas, Jeremy, and the luggage on the sidewalk. He didn't want to think about the struggle Thomas could have had trying to tell the driver they had to wait for him.

On the way to the airport he saw the cabdriver watching them in the rearview mirror, watching them sign in silence except for the occasional involuntary grunt or squeak deaf people couldn't hear themselves make. Theo wanted to say, "What do you care how we talk to each other, huh? I bet you don't even speak English either." But he kept himself quiet. The mood he was in was black enough without insulting an innocent solid citizen.

Jeremy loved to fly. He loved being above the clouds, alone with his father and big brother, going somewhere interesting. He loved the endless Cokes and peanuts and little souvenir wings. He even loved the silent vibration of the plane through the seat of his pants. He was fun to travel with, if one was in the right frame of mind.

Theo was not in the right frame of mind. Because Palma was waiting for him in Boston, and Ivy wasn't waiting for him in Philadelphia.

In Boston, they got a cab at the airport, but it was seven o'clock on a Friday evening, the beginning of the Labor Day weekend, and the traffic was beyond hellacious. Naturally, they were late, arriving at the gallery just seconds before the opening officially began, though there were already a lot of people there, gathered in intent clumps around Palma's sculptures.

Palma ran toward them as they came in the door, and Theo could tell from the look on her face that she was balanced between concern for their tardiness and the opportunity for drama that their entrance gave her. The draperies of her gown fluttered around her as she ran, aqueous shades of blue and gray, making her look as if she were running faster than she actually was. Her hands flashed, **Where have you been? I've been out of my mind. Did you bring the things I forgot? Oh, Jeremy, your shirttail is out. Thomas, why don't you notice these things?**

At the same time that she was fussing over them, she was herding them toward the gallery owner and a clutch of people standing with champagne glasses in their hands around the sculpture titled *Spirit*.

Theo had to admit, it was beautiful: a stylized pair of hands, cast in silvery stainless steel, in the midst of making the sign for *spirit*, or *ghost*. It would be beautiful even if you didn't know that the position of the hands had meaning; even if you didn't know that the silvery objects *were* hands. Palma had captured a grace and fluidity, an emotion and an impact that had universal appeal. The fact that she was deaf and actually communicated with the signs that she made art from had given her a credibility, a renown, and a bankability that were unique. And she'd taken to her fame effortlessly, accepting it as no less than what was due her.

Theo knew the drill—he'd done it often enough. He stuck his hand out to the gallery owner, who took it and shook enthusiastically. "I'm Theo, Palma's oldest. This is Jeremy, my brother, and this is my father, Thomas Dennison." Once his hand was free, he signed introductions to Thomas and Jeremy. Then he knew he was stuck interpreting for the rest of the evening, in spite of the presence of the trained interpreter that Mr. Swick, the gallery owner, had hired for Palma.

Come help me, Theo, Palma signed. I want everybody to know this big handsome boy is my son. Just run brush your hair first. You look like you were pulled through a hedge backward.

Thanks, Mom, he thought, and went obediently off to brush his hair. Even in his present mood, he wasn't reckless enough to tangle with Palma about his hair on the first night of her show.

By the time the reception was over, and then the long dinner at the fancy restaurant, Theo was exhausted. He wished he could slump over, suddenly asleep, the way Jeremy had, but he had to keep pushing himself along, interpreting for Palma and Thomas with the art world hotshots who were picking up the check. No one seemed to understand what strenuous work interpreting was—not just physically, though there was that, having one's arms in motion all the time—but mentally, too. Poor translating could make his parents seem slow or dull, which he didn't want to do, no matter how annoyed he was with Palma. The grammar and syntax of American Sign Language were completely different from those of English, and the effort of switching back and forth, searching for the most precise sign, the most exact word, was taxing and sometimes impossible. It was especially so toward the end of the evening, when Theo's brain abruptly went into vapor lock and nothing seemed to work. He'd stop, his hands in the air, every eye on him, and be unable to think of any way to go on.

"I'm sorry," he said. "I'm just blanking." He felt literally blank, which is what he knew an interpreter should be in order to serve only as a conduit, an instrument of translation. But after hours of such work, he felt lonely and somehow erased.

You're tired, Thomas signed. **Time to go.**

Theo was easily able to translate that, though he made it seem that they were all tired from a day of so much excitement and success. Three of Palma's sculptures had sold on the spot, and there was interest in several others.

As Theo expected, Palma decided to stay on a few more days instead of returning home with them on Monday evening. She liked hanging around the gallery, checking out the buyers of her work, being fussed over, taken to lunch and dinner. He was glad to kiss her goodbye and pass her off to the professional interpreter when the Posse got in the taxi for the airport. His mood was only marginally better than it had been on the way into town Friday, though Thomas and Jeremy were as zippy as ever.

I liked the subway, Jeremy signed.

No kidding, Thomas answered. **We only had to ride it a hundred times. Just like we do at home.**

I can't help it if I like all subways. You liked it, too, Jeremy signed. **You can't fool me.**

Too true. Never could. How about you, Theo? What did you like best?

I don't know. In order not to be such a lunk, he worked to come up with something. **Just walking around, I guess. Looking at all the people.**

There were some interesting-looking ones, that's for sure. Which one was your favorite?

He thought hard and came up with one. **The guy on**

the corner by the hotel—the one who wasn't really begging, just offering advice for sale.

Did he give you any?

Just a tidbit. He wouldn't tell me the rest unless I gave him some money—and I didn't have any.

Well? What was the tidbit?

He said, Think very carefully before you . . .

Before you what?

I don't know. That's the part I had to pay for. Maybe it would have been, Think very carefully before you get mixed up with a purple-haired girl.

Well, here's my advice, Thomas signed, laughing. Think very carefully before you give money to some guy on a street corner. If his advice was any good, he wouldn't be on a street corner.

5

Back at school Tuesday morning, Theo didn't want to be looking for Ivy. If she was tight now with Claire Cassidy and that crowd, he might as well save his horsepower. He was the guy who was good at calculus, but who had something weird about his family. (He'd lost track of the number of times people had misunderstood him and said, "Your family is all *dead*?") He was the one who, all through elementary and middle school, had had to give a class report about sign language. And always, for a while afterward, everybody in his class knew how to sign *thank you* and *please,* and looked at him as if he'd dropped in from another solar system.

If Ivy had managed to avoid the trap of being known as the one with the deaf father, the one who was such a novelty because she knew sign language, then she was lucky. And she should make the most of it. If he could move to a new school in a new town the way she had, he'd make sure it was years before anybody knew he had deaf—not *dead* —parents.

She came up behind him, alone, when he was heading for the bus. "Hi. How was your weekend?"

He started so violently he almost dropped his books. "Jeez. You could have given me a heart attack. How about some warning next time?" He hoped it didn't show how glad he was to see her.

"Sorry," she said. "Sorry, sorry, sorry. I'll try again." She walked beside him for a few paces before she said, "Hi, Theo. Did you have a good weekend?"

"It was fine. How about you?"

"It was okay. I went to the zoo. I meant to get there all summer and never did."

"So, how did you like it?" Thomas had joined the Zoological Society when Theo was born and had taken him there hundreds of times. Theo never liked going as much as Thomas and Jeremy did, but he went anyway, to keep the Posse together. Besides, people thought you were odd if you didn't like zoos, and he already felt odd enough.

"Zoos make me sad," Ivy said. "No matter how beautiful or natural-looking the enclosure is, it's still a cage. I know some of those animals are endangered and wouldn't be surviving at all except for zoos, but I wonder what they'd say if you asked them. Maybe they'd rather be extinct than having to live their whole lives practically in a box."

He nodded. She was the first person he'd ever known

who admitted to feeling the same way he did. His heart stumbled a little in his chest. "The wolves are the worst for me," he said. "In the wild, they need forty miles to roam."

"Maybe extinction isn't the worst thing," Ivy said. "Maybe living a way you hate is. If you're extinct, you can be a beautiful memory instead of a pitiful reality."

They got on the bus and sat down together. Theo wanted to ask her who she'd gone with, but one, he couldn't make himself ask such a nosy question, and two, he wasn't completely sure he wanted to know.

As if she'd read his mind, she said, "I went with my dad. He needs to get out more. If I didn't drag him off to see the town he lives in, all he'd ever know about would be the house, his office, and the park where he goes to fly his model planes. He has *zero* curiosity about places. I don't get it—they're all so different and so interesting."

"You've lived a lot of places?"

"What's a lot? About six or seven, I guess. That's not much to some, a lot to others."

"To you is it a lot?" Was he babbling? He hoped not, but his internal climate had improved so dramatically now he knew she'd gone to the zoo with her father, and not with Claire Cassidy and her outfit, that he might be.

"Yeah, I guess. What happens is I feel at home everywhere at the same time that I don't really feel at home anywhere."

"Moving at the beginning of senior year must have been hard." Definitely babbling. Could she tell?

"Moving's always hard. But Dad says it got less hard when my mother left. She carried on like a banshee every time he got a better job and had to move on. She didn't seem to get the point that his better jobs were what let her quit working and do whatever she wanted to do."

Nobody'd ever talked to him this way—just straight out, telling the truth about their lives without seeming to think about what impression it would make on him. He'd never known anybody except for Jeremy, maybe, who was that natural. He sure hoped she didn't expect him to be able to do that, too.

"Am I wrong, or do I have the impression you didn't want people to notice you were signing with me last week?" she asked.

Signers were usually good at reading body language and faces, as well as just hands, but she'd seen more than he wanted her to. Now he had to answer her question, and apparently she did expect him to be as honest as she was.

"It makes me feel weird," he finally said, out loud for the first time in his life. "So *other*. I don't want to be known as that guy who can sign. It has nothing to do with who I am—it's just some . . . some artifact of who my parents are, something I couldn't help."

"If your first language was French instead of sign, would you feel the same way?" Her tone was simply curious.

He thought. "Maybe not as much. French isn't as obvious."

"You'd probably have an accent."

"Yeah, but that would be charming and interesting. Knowing how to sign is just weird. Because there's a weird reason why it's your first language—not just that you were born somewhere else."

"You think deafness is weird?"

"Yeah. Don't you?"

"I think it's a lot of things, but weird's not one of them."

"What is it, then?"

"Well. It's a shame, sometimes. I wish Dad could hear music, and go to the movies, and make an ordinary phone call. He says he doesn't mind—how can he, he's never known any different? But I mind for him. And it can be an economic hardship. Most deaf people aren't as lucky as Dad about jobs. They can't always get work doing what they're really qualified for. And it's a social problem, since deaf people have a hard time communicating with people who don't sign. And it's isolating, if there's no deaf community near you." Then, as if reluctant to admit it, she said, "And it can be inconvenient for a relative who knows how to sign." She looked out the window. "Hey! This is my stop."

She stood and squeezed by Theo, who was overly conscious of the back of her legs brushing his knees.

"See you tomorrow," she said over her shoulder as she headed down the aisle.

Everything she'd said about deafness was true, of course

it was, but that didn't change the fact that having two deaf parents and a deaf brother was a weird kind of life. Did she really not get that?

The next day, he saw her in the halls three times on the way to classes. Once she was alone, once with two girls he didn't know, and once with a guy who was on the tennis team. She smiled and said, "Hi, Theo," every time they passed.

He didn't want to see her with anybody else. He wanted her to walk with him. But it was clear to him that, with her finely polished adaptive skills and easy naturalness, she was somebody everybody would want to be friends with. Why should she pick him?

She wasn't on the bus that afternoon. Had she just missed it, or was the tennis star driving her home? Or maybe she'd gone to McDonald's with Claire Cassidy and her gang.

Or maybe she was just avoiding him. He had to calculate that possibility.

He'd never felt like this about a girl before, even when there had been ones he'd really liked. It couldn't just be the fact that they both had deaf parents. What kind of basis was that for a relationship? It wasn't just her purple hair and her calmness, either. Oh, it was all of that, but something more, too. Maybe that's what they called chemistry. Just his luck the only science he really understood was mathematics.

He got home to find the phone light blinking. He was tempted not to answer it, afraid it would be Palma with a set of long-distance instructions for him. But he knew himself too well. There might be somebody somewhere who could ignore a ringing telephone, but it wasn't him.

"Hi, Theo? It's Ivy."

"Uh," he said, too stunned for speech. His faith in always answering the phone had just been confirmed.

"You okay?"

"Sure. Yeah, I'm fine. What's up?"

"I've got to go to the supermarket. I thought maybe you'd like to go with me. Keep me company."

"The supermarket?"

"The place where you buy food. I'm sure you must have heard of it."

"I just meant—why the supermarket?"

"Well, I have to go or we won't be having any dinner tonight. And too, I felt like our conversation on the bus yesterday wasn't finished. You know—about deafness. So I thought maybe you'd be interested in finishing it." She paused. "But maybe not."

The phone wires hummed. The whole subject made him uncomfortable. On the other hand, he definitely wanted to see her.

"Okay," he said, finally filling the silence. "Sure, I'll go with you. Shall I meet you?"

"I'll come get you. What's your address?"

He told her.

"Be there in ten minutes." She hung up.

Grocery shopping. Well, that was a new one.

Luckily, Jeremy had soccer practice after school, so he wouldn't be home until five-thirty.

Theo ran up the stairs two at a time. He changed his shirt and brushed his hair, and then, deciding he might look as if he was trying too hard, changed back to the shirt he'd been wearing all day. He had to brush his hair again, and then he rumpled it so it wasn't obvious he'd just brushed it.

He was still fussing with himself, looking sideways in the mirror, when he heard a horn honk outside. He ran down the stairs, missing the last two entirely and almost falling to his knees. With his hand on the doorknob, he took a deep breath and put his shoulders back. For Pete's sake, it was only grocery shopping.

She beeped again as he opened the door and went out.

At the market, Ivy took a two-page list from her jeans pocket. "Let's go, big boy."

He grabbed a cart and followed her.

"Who are you cooking for, the Marines?"

"I like to cook." She stood weighing a tomato in her hand, then put it down for reasons he couldn't discern and put another one into a plastic bag.

"Your dad a big eater?"

"I could feed him Wheaties three times a day for years and he'd never know the difference. I don't cook just for us. I cook for other people, too." She added more tomatoes and twisted the bag closed.

"What, you mean like soup kitchens, the homeless, like that?"

"I've done that. But what I like more is sort of catering. It's more personal. I'm buying this"—she brandished an eggplant—"to make ratatouille for my neighbors."

"Make what?" What she'd said sounded like a swear word made up by a little kid.

"Ratatouille. It's a kind of vegetable stew. Delicious."

"Oh."

"What do you eat at your house?"

"When my dad is in charge, which is most of the time, it's pizza, and pizza with a side of pizza, or mac and cheese, or hamburgers. Stuff like that. When my mom's in the kitchen, which isn't her favorite thing, it's vegetables and skinless chicken breasts and tofu items. I can scramble eggs. Jeremy—that's my brother—can make toast. That's about it."

"I think your eating habits are weirder than all that stuff you think about being deaf, if you want to know the truth." She examined the eggplants as if they were diamonds.

"Okay. So maybe *weird* was the wrong word."

"*Other* was another way you put it."

"Well, *other* is probably closer."

"Don't you know everybody feels *other* in some way?" She put two eggplants in the cart and moved on to onions.

"Not as other as we are."

She looked him straight in the face. "I feel more other because of moving so much, not because Dad's deaf. He takes care of himself. I don't help him any more than family members *should* help each other. Especially since there's just the two of us, we look out for each other. So don't go trashing deaf people to me, please. I'm not interested."

He stood, staring at the pile of onions while she bagged some and moved on. Trashing? How about just having an opinion? And wasn't she the one who'd wanted to have this discussion?

He caught up with her and took her arm. She jerked it out of his grasp. A couple of other shoppers turned to look at them.

"Don't manhandle me, okay?" she said.

He held both hands up, palms facing her. "Sorry."

She threw zucchini into a bag without looking at them. Or at him.

"Hey." He leaned close to her and spoke in her ear, aware that at least one shopper was still watching him suspiciously. "What was that all about?"

"I just didn't think *you*, of all people, would think that way about deaf people. It's bad enough I have to keep explaining and soothing and clarifying to other people about deafness and signing and all that—I thought with you I'd be able to just relax about it, but here you are, giving me trouble, too. It's just way too much." She wheeled the cart away from him and whipped off down the aisle.

Fine, he thought. His instincts were pulling him in one direction while his hormones pulled him in another. The hell with the hormones. He had enough aggravation in his life already. He didn't need some girl who got upset so easily. And lucky for him, he had his bus pass in his pocket.

All the way home, he steamed. Since when couldn't a guy have an opinion? Without coming right out and saying it, she'd pretty much admitted having a deaf parent was a nuisance, too. Still, he knew he'd done something big-time wrong in Ivy's book, and no matter how justified he believed he was, he felt like a worm.

When he came walking down the sidewalk from the bus stop toward his house, he saw Ivy's car parked at the curb. What—did she want to go another round with him? No, thank you. He wasn't interested in getting an eggplant between the eyes.

She was leaning against the side of the car, her arms folded, when he walked by. "Hey," she said.

"Hey yourself." He kept walking.

She straightened up. "I was out of line," she said. "You're entitled to have any opinion you want."

"Gee, thanks." But he stopped, standing sideways to her, not looking at her—but stopped all the same.

"So sue me." Her voice had a touch of vinegar in it

again. "I was looking for a friend. Somebody who'd know what it was like."

"You have an interesting way of making friends."

She walked around to the driver's side of the car. "Never mind."

"Wait." The word came out of his mouth completely involuntarily. What did he want her to wait *for*?

She stopped. "What?"

"What about Claire Cassidy? What about Mr. Tennis? You've got friends."

She opened the car door. "Last I heard, you could have more than two. Excuse me for thinking you could be one." She got in the car and slammed the door.

While Theo was still trying to figure out what had happened, she drove off.

Jeremy came around the corner dragging his backpack, his soccer cleats clattering on the cement. He waved to Theo and, when he reached him, dropped his backpack and signed, **What are you doing out on the sidewalk?**

Nothing.

Jeremy shrugged, signed, **I need food**, picked up his backpack, and headed for the house.

Food, thought Theo. What a troublemaker it was. All his problems with Ivy had started at the supermarket.

6

He was still trying to get a handle on what had happened with Ivy the next day when she passed him in the hall, handed him a plastic bag without a word, and kept going.

The bag was full of cookies. He hesitated briefly, wondering if they might be poisoned, figured he was overreacting, and took one out of the bag. It was round and thick and dark brown, sprinkled with little square grains of sugar. It gave off scents of cinnamon and molasses. He bit into it.

Oh, my God. His mouth was clicking its heels, jumping with flavors, celebrating. This was the taste of joy. Of rhapsodies. Of love.

What was she, some kind of multiple personality, slamming doors on him one minute and wooing him with unbelievable food the next? Did she do the same thing for Claire Cassidy and Mr. Tennis?

Who cared, he thought, polishing off the rest of the cookies in the bag, as long as she kept bringing him food.

After school, she was waiting for him at the bus stop. "Hi," she said.

"Hi," he said warily.

"So?"

He just looked at her.

"The cookies," she said. "Did you like them?"

He closed his eyes in blissful memory.

"Awesome. Phenomenal. Stellar. You got any more?" It was hard to recall how she'd treated him the day before while he thought about the cookies.

"Males are so simple," she said. "All appetite."

"Pitiful but true," he said. "You got any more?"

"How soon do you want them?"

"Immediately?"

"You want to come home with me?"

Whoa—what was happening now? Was she setting him up for some other blunder that he'd inadvertently make but never understand? He didn't know whether to be relieved or disappointed that he couldn't take her up on her invitation. "Sorry. Can't. Jeremy's going to be home soon, and my mom gets back tonight. We have to shovel out the place."

She gave him a long look, and then said, "Okay. I'll bring you some more tomorrow."

"Great." He wanted to ask her why, but didn't.

On the bus, he was spared having to decide whether to sit next to her by the fact that there weren't two seats together. She sat four rows ahead of him and he watched the purple strand of her hair swing as she talked to the guy next to her. When she rose at her stop, she looked back at him and waved. He waved, too. She signed, **Cookies**, and got off.

They met Palma at the airport after dinner.

She was exhausted and distracted. Traveling without an interpreter was difficult for her, and the trip home lacked the excitement and anticipation of the trip out. In addition, the fussing over her was finished, and she had nothing to look forward to but the ordinariness of her own family, and months of work before she got any more fanfare.

Sold them all, she signed before slumping into the front seat, her head back and her eyes closed.

Thomas drove, now and then taking his big hand off the wheel to pat Palma's, which lay limp and open on the seat beside her. Once home, Palma trudged wearily upstairs, dragging her shawl behind her, while Thomas and Theo, well trained, lugged her suitcases.

As the Posse sat downstairs watching the captions on TV, Palma lay heavily asleep overhead. Theo thought he could feel the actual weight of her and all her expectations pressing upon him through the ceiling.

. . .

He looked for Ivy all day at school and not just because of the cookies. But he never saw her. Was she hiding from him, playing some kind of mind game he was too dumb to catch on to, enjoying making him squirm? He found himself finger-spelling, **What? Why?** and made himself stop. No matter how many questions he asked himself, he drew a blank on answers.

When he got home, there was a message on the answering machine from her. "Sorry about the cookies. I had to help Dad out at a seminar and luncheon, so I didn't make it to school. But the cookies are here in the kitchen if you want to come and get them." And she'd added her address.

He found Palma in the living room, where she was sitting in a chair looking blankly out the window.

I have to go out. Jeremy'll be home from Kevin's about five-thirty. I'll be home in time for dinner.

He decided to give himself plenty of leeway, though in actuality he might be home in fifteen minutes.

Palma nodded, not even going to the trouble to sign, **Okay.**

She was often like this after a show: let-down and depleted, sure she'd never sculpt anything interesting again, even though her inspiration was literally at her fingertips all the time. The odds of her making any dinner were pretty dim, too. When she was dispirited she wasn't hungry, and she didn't think anybody else should be, either. As usual, Thomas would somehow pick up the slack. Fleetingly, Theo, before the pull of Ivy and her cookies got him out the door, wondered if that ever got old.

He rode his bike to Ivy's rather than get into a discussion with Palma about borrowing her car. Though she hardly ever drove it, preferring to have somebody else do the driving, she was still intensely possessive about it. Yet there were times when she'd practically fling it at him, all generosity and goodwill and maternal indulgence. But then other times when she was all suspicion and reluctance and criticism. He didn't want to take a chance on this being one of those times.

From the front door he followed Ivy back to the kitchen, where she resumed stirring something in a big kettle on the stove. She wore a blue chef's apron and was steeped in an aroma that was warm and steamy and delicious.

"What's in the pot?" he asked.

"Butter and carrots and leeks. For soup for my ladies."

"Your ladies?"

"Well, there are a couple of gents, too, but mostly it's ladies who live around here. Our neighborhood has a lot of old folks, almost all of them living alone, and they're tired of cooking, or they don't like it. Which I do. So I cook for them and they pay me. It works out for all of us."

"How'd that get started?" He was eyeing the plate of cookies on the kitchen table, but didn't want to appear overeager.

"At the beginning of the summer, right after we moved in, I was cooking when this old couple came to the door collecting for something, heart or TB or some disease that's not as stylish as AIDS or cystic fibrosis, and they smelled what I was cooking and got to salivating. So I asked them in to have some, since I didn't have any money to give them, and it turned out they were a brother and sister who lived next door to each other. Both their spouses had died and they thought about living together, but they valued their privacy too much and also they fought too much, just like when they were little kids. So they bought adjoining houses and they ate together a lot. But neither of them were good cooks. Harry, the brother, says cooking's what he misses most about his wife. And he says that Hazel—that's the sis-ter—Hazel's cooking is probably what did her husband in. So they made me a deal—that I'd cook supper for them four nights a week, and one of those nights I'd cook enough for them to have friends over. So now I cook for a few of the friends, too. Go ahead and have some cookies. I can tell I won't have your full attention until you do."

He didn't need to be told twice. "Oh, my God," he said, with his mouth full. "What are these?"

"They're toasted coconut cookies. Do you have to eat two at once?"

"Yes," he mumbled, reaching for two more.

She took a glass from the cupboard and handed it to him. "Get some milk, for goodness' sake, before I have to do CPR on you for choking. It would be embarrassing to have to tell Hazel that my cooking, too, was responsible for a death."

He washed the cookies down with milk and then had more of both.

"Did you know that Napoleon ate in eight minutes when he dined alone?"

He shook his head, his mouth too full to respond, but what could he say to that, anyway? How would anybody know how fast Napoleon ate? More to the point, who would care?

"He slowed down when he had company. It took him twelve minutes to eat then." She poured stock into the soup pot.

He swallowed. "How do you know?"

"I'm not just some brainless cook, you know. I'm a food historian as well. What's been more vital to the survival of the species—any species, if you get right down to it—than food? Famine can lead to the extinction of whole peoples. Or to their migration. Or to wars to get fertile territory that belongs to somebody else. The search for spices motivated Columbus and a bunch of other great explorers. In the 1600s the Caribbean sugar plantations started a slave trade for field workers. Food's not just cookies and milk so you can have an afternoon snack. It's social, it's political, it's spiritual."

Well, he could think of something else that was just as vital to the survival of the species, but he sure wasn't going to get into that with her. "You mean somebody was timing Napoleon while he ate?"

"Evidently. And that fact is not just some interesting trivia, in case that's what you were thinking." She raised an eyebrow at him as if she knew exactly what was in his mind. "It's revealing about his personality. Eating wasn't a pleasure for him, it was a necessity, something to be gotten out of the way so he could get on to bigger things. He was a guy in a hurry."

"So you think the way he always had his hand inside his coat, maybe he had heartburn?"

She laughed. "Could be." She peeled a potato, sliced it, and added it to the pot.

"About the other day . . ." she began.

He stopped chewing for a moment. He didn't think he wanted to get into that conversation again. It hadn't ended so well the last time.

He gave her a wary look and slowly began chewing again.

She peeled another potato. "I guess I got so upset because . . . because part of me agreed with what you were saying. And I didn't want to." She finished speaking in a rush.

When he didn't say anything, she went on.

"It *is* weird being the kid of a deaf person. As normal as it is most of the time, sometimes it's weird. And no matter how much you tell yourself that every member in every family is supposed to care for the other members, and look out for them, there are still times when having to do things for deaf parents goes above and beyond that." She put down the potato. "A guy I knew in Seattle, he had to interpret for his parents when they were getting divorced. He couldn't even pay attention to how upset he was because he had to make sure they both understood what their lawyers were saying."

Theo shook his head and made a sound, but he didn't know the right words to say.

"I've heard about kids who had to interpret embarrassing doctor visits for their parents when they were too young to have to know about certain body-part problems, if you get my drift. That definitely qualifies as weird." She started peeling the potato again. "But I don't want to feel sorry for myself, or get resentful of my dad for something he can't help. So sometimes I just . . . I don't know . . . deny stuff, I guess."

He took a big gulp of milk. "I wish I *could* deny stuff. It's in my face all the time, especially with Palma. And I do resent it."

"Palma?" She sliced the potato and dropped it in the pot.

"My mother. Talk about your basic easy-to-lip-read name."

"Your mom is Palma Dennison?"

Well, of course Ivy would know Palma's name. She was famous enough in the hearing world, but among deaf people she was practically a goddess.

"The one and only."

"Oh, wow. I love her work." She shot him a look. "And not just because she's deaf. It's beautiful. My favorites are the little green ones. What does she make those out of?"

"Chalcedony." This was one of the many times he wished he had a mother nobody had ever heard of, one whose biggest accomplishment was being PTA president. Okay, yeah, he was proud of her. He liked her work. He benefited from it. But nothing about her life was normal. She worked in a frenzy, sometimes all night long; she couldn't care less about taking care of the family laundry or grocery shopping or making dinner or bill-paying or getting gas in the car—the stuff that *had* to be done to keep the show on the road—but she sure as hell wanted somebody else to do it so that things went smoothly for her. The person she thought of first almost every minute of every day was herself, and what she thought about was what she wanted. Her being deaf was only part of what made his life odd.

"Well, I love those. Someday I hope I can afford one. You resent *her*?"

"Don't you know her picture's next to the words *prima donna* in the dictionary? She'd be a handful even if she wasn't deaf."

"But she must be able to hire interpreters. What do you have to resent?"

"She doesn't want to hire interpreters. She doesn't like having to explain herself to a different person every time. And even when she does get somebody else to do any kind of work for her, she's not the easiest person to work for. They usually don't want to do it again no matter how famous she is. Besides, she wants me. To her, there's no such thing as its being inconvenient for me."

Ivy stirred the pot and put the lid on it. "What about your dad?"

"He's just the opposite. He hates to ask me for help. He'll even go to the doctor by himself and miss half of what the doctor tells him because he doesn't want to be a bother to me. And his speech is so good, because he wasn't deafened until he was eight, that people don't realize he's as handicapped as he is."

"He lets you use that word, *handicapped*?"

"I don't know. I never use it in front of him. But I know all about how most deaf people don't want to be considered handicapped. But, dammit, they are. What about that seminar of your dad's today? You had to leave school for it. He couldn't go without help."

"He usually gets an interpreter for stuff like that. There

was some glitch today, that's all. He doesn't like me to miss school for him."

"But my point is, he needed help for an ordinary part of life. In my book, that's handicapped, no matter how proud you are of your culture and your language and all that. It's the same as if they spoke only French, to use your example. They still need help in ordinary situations because they don't speak the same language as everybody else living here. If that's not a handicap, what is? But don't use that word around Palma. You'll get your head handed to you."

"How come you call her Palma and not Mom?"

"She likes Palma better. Says it expresses her personality better. Her identity is not described by being a mom. Stuff like that."

"Oh." She peeked at the soup and put the lid back on. "This soup has to simmer for a while. You want to see Dad's airplanes?"

"Sure." He was glad to be through with talking about Palma. He followed Ivy to an extra bedroom at the back of the house. It had been fitted out as a workshop, and on the long table across the far wall were two planes under construction. From the ceiling hung completed models, perfect right down to the tiny pilot in the cockpit.

"I'd be afraid to fly these," he said. "It'd be a tragedy to crack one up."

"Not a total tragedy. Because then he gets to rebuild it.

Most of the fun, at least for him, is in the building, not the flying."

"They're as much works of art as the stuff Palma does."

"He'd love to hear you say that. He thinks so, too."

"You have any interest in making them?"

"Not the slightest. You want to be a sculptor?"

"Not for any amount of money."

"So, what's your thing?"

He went over to the workbench and ran his hand lightly over the sleek body of a plane. "Numbers do it for me. They're so neat. No loose ends. Laws that always work. Beauty in precision."

"Don't you find people boring who don't have a passion?" she asked, watching him. "Don't you think that's what brings them to life?"

He'd never thought about that before. He'd never really thought of mathematics as a passion, either. It was just something he liked, something he was good at. But now he understood that it *was* his passion—the thing he wanted to keep doing all his life.

"I always want to know what people think about when they're falling asleep at night," Ivy said. "If it's the same thing most nights, then I know what their passion is. Or if they even have one. And then I know if I'm going to like them."

Suddenly, he was proud of mathematics, proud that it

was his passion, proud that he often fell asleep running formulas through his head. It didn't matter that Palma thought mathematics was boring, useless, incomprehensible. It didn't matter that she couldn't see why he wanted to go to MIT, why he couldn't just live at home and go to Penn or Drexel. If you had a passion, you didn't have to explain it, you just had to do it. The way Palma made shapes out of wet clay, or Ivy's father built airplanes just to see them crack up. Or Ivy and her ratatouille.

"I'd better check on the soup," Ivy said. "If it boils over, it can bake into ceramics on a stovetop before you know what happened. Do you think we're stereotypes?"

Oh, man, she was losing him again. "Stereotypes?"

"Yeah, you know, gender stereotypes. I'm the girl, so I cook, and you're the guy, so you do math."

"Looks like it from the outside, I guess." Every time he talked to her, he could almost feel his brain stretching. "But you're a historian, too. And I do math because I like it, not because I think it's manly. In fact, it's probably pretty nerdy. And you cook because you like it, not because the culture says you should. You could live on Wheaties if you wanted to."

She gave him a smile that spotlighted her show-stopping dimple.

In the kitchen, the soup was still in the pot, not on the stove, and it smelled like comfort and joy.

"You want to take some home?" she asked. "I'm making a big batch. It'll be a nice change from pizza."

"Sure. Thanks." Even though he was full of cookies, Theo's mouth watered for the soup. He wondered what she'd been cooking the day Harry and Hazel showed up. What had been the aroma that had pulled them inside?

"I made these little round loaves of bread to serve it in. Let me give you some of those, too. Then all you need is a salad—and you must have someone at home who can make one of those. And here are some toasted coconut cookies for dessert." She was arranging things in bags and jars when he got it: she really was a professional, working at her passion. She wasn't just some kid with a cute hobby.

On the ride home, the bag dangling from the handlebars, he realized that they were friends once more. And he had no idea how it had happened. He was just glad that it had.

7

Somehow he was back in her kitchen again a couple of afternoons later, watching her take roasted chickens, and potatoes with rosemary and garlic, and butternut squash with walnuts and lime juice out of the oven. It gave him the same feeling he got when he watched his father do a magic trick that was inexplicable enough to be real magic.

"How do you think this stuff up?" he asked.

"I don't know. I just imagine what would taste good together and then I try it out. How do you—well, whatever it is mathematicians do?"

"Pretty much the same." He picked up the last of the cheese straws from the bowl on the table.

"I must admit I'm baffled about some food choices. Like artichokes. Whoever figured out you could eat one of those? I guess you'd really have to be starving. And rancid fat—how did the Inuit learn they could get high on that?"

"Rancid fat?" He put the cheese straw back in the bowl.

"Yeah. Supposedly it gives the same effect you can get from beer or wine or gin. But I'm not going to try it out. Now come here and make yourself useful. You think I'm going to let you sit around here eating everything in sight while I do all the work?"

"I was hoping that would be the arrangement," he said.

"Well, think again, big boy. We're going to start packaging. See those foil containers?"

She bossed him around as if he were a not-too-bright little kid while he struggled to prove that she was wrong.

When they had everything boxed up, she said, "Now you're going to help me deliver it. This is Harry and Hazel's night to get extra, and they're having a bunch for supper. Some of their guests are my regular customers, but they're eating it tonight at Harry and Hazel's."

"Okay, what should I do?"

"Carry this stuff out to the car. I'll open the trunk."

It didn't even occur to him to resist her.

Harry and Hazel were waiting for them at Harry's house. They took turns hosting the weekly dinner party, and it was his turn. Their houses were connected brick row houses with geranium-filled window boxes, but the inside of Harry's was a surprise. It was as tidy as a ship and filled with maritime artifacts—brass navigational instruments and framed sea charts on the walls, photos of rocky coastlines and dramatic seascapes, ship models on the mantel. It was no struggle for Theo to guess what Harry's passion was.

"Harry, this is my friend Theo. He's helping me today."

Harry was a short, solid man with the toughness and dimensions of a tree trunk. He was deeply tanned, with a ruffle of white hair around the edges of his skull and dark blue eyes set in a nest of wrinkles. He took Theo's hand in his big mitt and gave it a couple of hard shakes.

"Any pal of Ivy's has got to be okay," he said, "because she's a genius."

"That's right," Ivy said, laying containers out on the kitchen counter. "And don't you forget it."

"No way," he said, letting go of Theo's hand. "Not when I remember how well fed I am."

"Six for dinner, right?"

"We-e-ell, maybe eight."

Ivy laughed. "I figured. So I brought extra. You always do that. You must know—and I forget who said this—that the best dinner parties are no fewer than five or more than nine: more than the Graces and fewer than the Muses."

Hazel, small-boned and quick, with improbably red hair in tight curls, had been peeking into bags and boxes. "Oooh—are these those coconut things? I love those. Maybe I'll just keep them all for myself and give the guests some ice cream."

"No you don't, Hazy," Harry said. "You can do whatever

you want next door, but in my house, the guests get the good stuff."

"Oh, all right," she pouted. Theo saw that she'd sneaked a cookie from the bag and slipped it into her pocket.

"Now say hello to Ivy's friend."

"Hello, dear," Hazel said obediently. "Are you a cook, too?"

"Right," Theo said. "My specialty is ice cubes. We have a recipe that's been in the family for generations."

Harry guffawed. "I'll match mine against yours anytime. There's an art to it, isn't there?"

"No doubt about it."

Ivy turned from the counter and signed to Theo, **Get to work, big boy. There's more stuff in the car to unload."**

"Okay, okay," he signed.

"Hey," Harry said, "what was that about?"

"Oh, she just told me to get back to work and quit sharing culinary secrets."

"Told you? I didn't hear her say a word."

Without realizing they were doing it, Theo and Ivy had communicated in sign.

"It was sign language, Harry," Ivy said. "We've both got deaf parents, so we're bilingual. And it sure comes in handy when you want to tell secrets."

"You're not just whistling Dixie," he said. "Hey, Hazy,

wouldn't you like to know how to do that so you and your pals could gossip in church? And you and I could talk over our back fences without yelling at each other." He turned to Ivy. "Say, Ivy. You think I'm too old to learn how to do that? How do you say *old* in sign language?"

Ivy circled her right hand at her chin and pulled down as if she were stroking a beard.

Harry laughed and imitated her. "That's pretty good. Well, I may be"—he signed old—"but I don't want to act old. Learning something new is a good way to stay—how do you do *young*?"

Ivy grinned and placed the fingertips of her open hands just below her shoulders and moved them up and down several times.

Harry copied her and laughed again. "It makes me feel . . . young . . . just to do that. Come on, Hazy. Do this." He signed, old, young.

Hazel hesitantly copied Harry's motions, but quickly was doing them easily.

Then Ivy had to teach them the signs for *soup* and *cookie* and *party*.

While she did, Theo hung back by the door, watching and feeling uneasy for a reason he couldn't understand. What did he care if Harry and Hazel wanted to learn a few words of sign language? Hell, he wished everybody in the world would learn to sign and then nobody would need an interpreter. He'd be out of a job, and glad of it. But somehow it made him angry, watching Harry and Hazel play with his language as if it were a game, a novelty.

Ivy taught them *thank you* and *goodbye* and told them to have fun as she hauled Theo back to the car.

"Okay, what's going on with you?" she asked, once the doors were shut. "What's with that look on your face?"

"What do you mean? That's just how my face looks."

"Oh, don't give me that. It's about Harry and Hazel wanting to learn to sign, isn't it? Why didn't you like that?" She started the car and pulled out of the driveway.

He didn't want to tell her, didn't want to start up that old argument, but somehow he erupted with it anyway. "It's not a game! It's somebody's life! It's . . . it's like playing with someone's heart! With their brain!" He slumped back against the seat, feeling foolish and childish for his outburst. It didn't even make sense to him, so how must it sound to her?

She was quiet for a minute. "Would you have felt that way if I'd been teaching them a few words of French? I don't think so. And yet their language is that important to the French. They don't even want to let any English words creep in, like *le weekend* or *le drugstore* or *les bluejeans*. What's the difference?"

He thought of his father's callused hands signing in his strong, blunt way, of those same hands pulling an ace of hearts from Jeremy's ear or wielding a power saw. Those hands were not just language—they were life.

Palma's hands, too—long-fingered and elegant, her signing so much more refined than Thomas's, just as styles of oral speech could be different—a whole range of personality and sensitivity revealed in the movements of hands.

He let out a long breath. "I don't know. Signing just seems more important. More . . . more *integral.* Don't you feel it, too?"

"Yes," she said slowly. "But I'm not any better at saying it than you are. But what if Harry and Hazel really do want to learn to sign, not just to play with it? That would be good, wouldn't it?"

"But why would they? What are they going to do with it?"

"Gossip in church? Talk over the back fence? Challenge themselves to learn something new? What do you care? The more people who can sign, the better, that's what I think. Then it's easier for deaf people. Did you know that not all that long ago almost everybody on Martha's Vineyard could sign? Because they were so isolated, there was a lot of intermarrying, and that produced a lot of deaf people. So lots of hearing people who were relatives or friends of the deaf people learned to sign, too, and so shopkeepers and service people could communicate easily with them, and with each other. Wouldn't that be good right here?"

"Like that could ever happen."

"But why discourage even the few who want to learn? There might still be a few very old-timers on the Vineyard who aren't deaf but can sign. And you know what they probably use it for? To say things they don't want anybody else to catch on to. Don't tell me you've never done that."

He grunted, not wanting to let on that she made sense.

"I know, I know," she said when he remained quiet. "It's not *just* a language. It's much more personal. When you think of all the other things you do with your hands, it's such an extension of—oh, I don't know how to describe why signing's different from other kinds of language. It just is."

"And knowing it can be such a major pain, too," he said, slouched in his seat, his arms folded across his chest. "When you were a little kid, did you ever try to call for your parents at night when you woke up from a nightmare?"

She pulled up in front of his house and turned off the car. "Yeah."

"And what happens when you call for a deaf parent? With your voice or with your hands? Nothing. And what happens when you go into their bedroom in the dark and try to tell them in sign what's happened? Nothing."

She looked at her hands on the steering wheel. "I used to call for my mother, while she was still around, and you know what would happen? Nothing. And she could hear."

Why couldn't he remember that not all problems in deaf families could be blamed on deafness?

8

As September went on, he changed his habits, rushing for the first bus so he could get home in time to take care of Palma's phone calls and questions and errands and Jeremy's homework and still have time to stop in at Ivy's for even just a little while, to sit with her while she cooked, or help her deliver her Flying Food, as she called it. Sometimes he'd just sit at the kitchen table doing his homework while she stirred and measured and offered him tastes. Watching Ivy work with an intensity that paralleled Palma's, Theo learned that turmoil and drama didn't have to accompany the creative process. The way Ivy did it, there was pleasure and harmony and fun. It was a revelation to him, and a relief.

And he learned a lot from her food history facts. When he took offense at her calling him a parasite when he had to taste everything she made, she told him that in Roman times a parasite was a professional guest who, in exchange for the host's food, told stories, jokes, gossip, and the latest news, as well as laughed at all the host's jokes.

"You can eat all you want as long as you laugh at my jokes," she said. "Just be glad you're not living in the Middle Ages, when gluttony was one of the Seven Deadly Sins. And in Scotland, it wasn't just a sin, it was a crime. You could have been strangled or drowned for eating that whole bowl of caramel corn."

When he referred to somebody as a lady, being mildly insulting, she informed him that in Old English the word *lady* meant someone who made bread, and that it was a good thing to be, and that he could call her Lady Ivy if he ever wanted any of her homemade bread again.

He didn't know what to say when she told him that in the 1890s Parisian women used to go to slaughterhouses to get a glass of blood to drink. They thought it was a good tonic.

One afternoon, as Theo was getting ready to leave for Ivy's, Jeremy grabbed him around the legs. He let go long enough to sign, **Don't go**, and then grabbed on again.

They'd both had only a half day at school because of some teachers' conference, and he was anxious to get going, to have more time with Ivy. But he made himself sit down on the floor and face Jeremy. **Why?**

You're never here. You never do anything with me anymore except check my homework. Palma's no fun. She works all the time.

He'd been enjoying himself, and Jeremy had been pay-ing. He'd forgotten for a time, such a short, carefree time, that his obligations needed to come first, not his pleasure.

You want to come with me? I'm going to visit a girl who's the best cook in the world.

In the whole world?

I wouldn't be surprised. She always has cookies.

Let's go, Jeremy signed.

"Well, hi," Ivy said when she opened the door to Theo and Jeremy. "Who's this?"

J-e-r-e-m-y, Theo signed. **My brother.**

Hi, Jeremy. Come on in.

"I hope it's okay I brought him," Theo said. "He was bored and I told him you make the best cookies in the world and—"

"It's okay," she said, leading them back to the kitchen. "I'm always envious of people who have siblings. I like to see them together, even when they tell me they're envious of me being an only child."

"I'm envious of you being an only child," Theo said, and Ivy gave him one of her great smiles.

Have a seat, she signed to Jeremy. **I doubt you like cookies. Hardly anybody does. But there's a plate of them on the table, and my feelings will be hurt if you don't have at least one.**

Jeremy looked uncertainly at Theo.

She's kidding, Theo signed. **Dig in.**

Jeremy gave Ivy a quick glance, but she had her back turned, stirring something in a big bowl. He shoved a whole cookie in his mouth and signed, **How come she can sign?**

She has a deaf father, Theo signed. **And aren't you lucky you know the only language that allows you to talk with your mouth full.**

Sorry, Jeremy signed, taking another cookie. Theo had one, too, and got up to get them some milk. "What do you call these?" he asked Ivy.

"Toffee bars. You want to help me deliver? It's beef stroganoff and coleslaw."

"Sure. Jeremy'll have to go, too."

"Maybe not. My dad had a meeting canceled, so he's here this afternoon working on his planes. Do you think Jeremy'd like to help?"

"How would your dad feel about that?"

"He'd love it. He's been trying for years to get me interested, and it just doesn't float my boat." **Hey, Jeremy.** She tapped him on the shoulder. **You want to see something really cool?**

He nodded, his eyes big. A couple of Ivy's cookies had already convinced him that she was a person to be trusted, as well as worshipped. He got up and followed her down the hall like a devoted puppy.

Dr. Roper's worktable faced the door, the same way Palma's did, so he could see anybody who came in. People who couldn't hear didn't like to be surprised from behind. Probably nobody did.

Dr. Roper looked up, and Theo saw that he was indeed an extraordinarily good-looking man. Ivy had his dark hair and eyes, but not the perfect symmetry of his features. Which Theo thought made her face much more interesting than one that was merely flawless.

Ivy introduced Jeremy and Theo.

So this is Theo, Dr. Roper signed back.

The one and only, Theo signed, and wondered what Ivy had been saying about him.

Jeremy, who was used to crowding next to Thomas in his home workshop, always curious about what he was working on, edged up to the worktable. **What are you making?** His eyes were all over the place, taking in the blades, files, pliers, tweezers, and plane parts.

A Bristol M-1C. From World War I. When I'm done, I'll fly it.

It'll fly?

Soon as I get the motor in it. You ever flown a model airplane?

Jeremy pressed closer. **No. It's a beauty.**

Come over on this side. I'll show you what I'm trying to do.

Jeremy was there in an instant. The two of them bent their heads together over the plane.

Ivy tapped her father, who looked up. **Theo and I have to go deliver.**

He nodded and flipped his hand at them, dismissing them as he turned back to the more urgent business of Jeremy and the Bristol M-1C.

"Was that a dirty trick?" Theo asked as they went down the hall.

"Dirty trick? Are you kidding? The two of them are in heaven. We could come back in four hours and I bet they'd be in exactly the same positions."

They made two stops where no one was home, but Ivy had keys to the back doors so she could leave the dinners in the refrigerators.

Then they went to the home of Adele and Rochelle Cooper. They were twins, both tall and streamlined in khaki trousers and white shirts, with gray curls cropped close to their heads, and black skin so smooth it was hard to believe that in a few weeks they would celebrate their seventy-third birthdays. The only difference between them apparent to Theo was that Rochelle wore glasses and Adele didn't. Neither one had ever married, but they'd had a hand in raising a flock of nieces and nephews, and they wanted to have a big birthday party that would include them all, as well as their mothers, fathers, husbands, wives, kids, and significant others. Ivy was going to cater it.

After she'd put the coleslaw and beef stroganoff in the

refrigerator, Ivy sat down with the two ladies at the kitchen table while Theo wandered around the immaculate house looking at the dozens of graduation pictures, new-baby pictures, wedding pictures, and everyday snapshots that covered the walls, tabletops, and mantelpiece.

They weren't just pretty pictures, either. One was of some kid just screaming his head off, eyes all squinched up and mouth wide open. Another was of two women arguing across a dinner table, one of them half standing, poking her finger at the other one. Theo liked this style of showing everything about how families were, not just the presentable parts—in front of the Christmas tree, on vacation at Disney World, beaming at somebody's graduation.

He wondered what it would be like to be a part of such a pack of people, having their bad times together as well as their good, with somebody else available to take up the slack if you couldn't or didn't want to, always with someone around to talk your problems over with. And to take your picture, even in your most unflattering moments.

"Honey," Theo heard Adele say to Ivy, "if we can't have a chocolate overdose on our birthday, when we gonna have one?"

"Okay," Ivy said, laughing. "Double-chocolate fudge cake it is. A turkey and a ham, some salads, and buttermilk corn bread. What else?"

"Oh, just bring along some of those dips and pâtés and little bites of things you're so good at," Rochelle said.

"Some of those mushrooms with the cheese and walnuts inside. I like those."

"Okay," Ivy said. "I'll surprise you. How many people?"

The sisters put their heads together, counting on their fingers. "Looks like about thirty-five," Adele finally said.

Ivy whistled. "This is going to cost you."

"What's money for," Rochelle said, "if you can't have a good time with it? And nobody we'd rather spend it on than our family. Now, young man," she said to Theo, who was blatantly eavesdropping while he looked at a framed black-and-white picture on the fireplace mantel of two girls in old-fashioned white dresses, with their arms around each other's waists. "You come sit down here with us and have some iced tea and tell us what you're up to."

Theo obediently did as he was told, while Adele put a tall glass of iced tea in front of him and refilled the other three from a pitcher. "What I'm mostly up to is being Ivy's vassal."

"That's true," Ivy said, "and he still needs a lot of training. But maybe that's because he's also a brilliant mathematician and he's going to go to MIT and invent some theory as good as Einstein's. Probably better."

"Well, that sounds real good," Adele said. "Our nephew, Sammy, he went to MIT. He's doing something about computers now and taking his money to the bank in a wheelbarrow, not that that means everything, you know."

"You think Sammy's happy, Adele?" Rochelle asked. "I

think he's a shade on the dog-weary side, and no way is he spending enough time at home. We need to have a talk with him."

"Now, Rochelle," Adele answered, "you know we keep quiet—at least until we think we *have* to speak up."

"Seems to me," Rochelle said, "that's just about any time we get an idea in our heads." And she laughed a laugh that made Theo have to join in.

"But I think you're right," Adele said. She turned to Theo. "You be careful," she said. "No matter how much smarter than Mr. Einstein you are, you better remember: family first, work second. Don't let them tell you any different, MIT or no MIT."

"Yes, ma'am," Theo said meekly, and drank his iced tea. But he wanted to tell them that if anybody already knew about family first, it was him.

Back in the car, he said, "Those ladies don't have to worry about how MIT's going to pollute my mind. Palma doesn't want me to go away to college, so MIT's not really in my future."

Ivy's eyebrows went up. "What's wrong with your mother? You *should* go to MIT. Or Cal Tech, or some kind of Tech. You're brilliant."

He felt a warmth blossom in his chest. She didn't know anything about math except how to double a recipe, but she thought he was brilliant! "My brilliance is certainly a fact," he admitted. "I can't argue with you on that. But

Palma doesn't agree. And she'd be the one writing the checks."

"Then you should get a scholarship," Ivy went on passionately. "Or a work-study. Or a loan. You *have* to be able to do what you're meant to do."

For some reason, he felt anger rising in him, anger at her. "What have you got against some place like Penn? It's good enough for your father, isn't it?"

She turned on him. "It's not the same, and you know it. He's in charge of this big special project. He's doing something he's particularly qualified to do. And the fact that he was able to get the best possible education for himself is what's allowing him to be the one to do this. You need the best preparation, too. It's for the rest of your life. You must know that. And as good as Penn is, it's not the best place for you. And don't tell me Palma can't afford it. I know what her stuff sells for."

"She doesn't want me to leave home. She says Jeremy needs me. And so does she."

Ivy's eyes blazed. "That's the most selfish thing I've ever heard. She got along without you before you were born. Before you were old enough to make phone calls. Who helped her then?"

Theo was silent. He'd never thought of that. But, knowing her, he'd bet there'd been somebody she'd been able to charm or bully or wheedle into doing for her the things she didn't want to do.

"I don't know. But isn't that what family is all about? In all the Hallmark cards and movies-of-the-week, that's how it works."

"Hallmark cards and movies-of-the-week are fiction. This is real life. And if families are supposed to make sure that everybody gets what's best for them, what about you? Who's helping you get what's best for you?" She was talking so intensely that she'd forgotten about driving, and the car had gradually slowed to about twelve miles an hour. She jumped when the car behind her honked. "Okay, okay," she said, speeding up. "Don't you know speed kills?"

They pulled into the driveway at Ivy's house. Abruptly, she put her head on her hands, which still gripped the steering wheel. "Sorry, sorry, sorry. I'm really sorry. I know it's not my business. You understand more about the situation than I do. I shouldn't interfere."

His anger evaporated, and he wanted to touch her. To put his hand on her back, or stroke her hair, rub the beads threaded along her purple strand.

"It's okay," he said. He wanted to tell her that he liked that she cared what happened to him even if he wasn't sure why she did—was it because she really liked him or because she was somebody who couldn't help taking care of other people? He wasn't so dense that he didn't understand about the significance of feeding people. It was about the most nurturing thing you could do. And making meals was a daily necessity, a daily commitment, not even in the same league as a good deed you just did once in a while.

All he could think to do was to say, "It's okay," again, but this time he did put his hand on her back. He could feel the bumps of her spine through her T-shirt. As he ran his hand down her backbone, he was fascinated by that warm, fragile column that kept so much energy going.

She turned her head to look at him, and he saw that her eyes were wet, her lashes stuck together in dark points.

"Hey," Theo said, startled and embarrassed. "Everything's cool. Really." But he kept his hand on her back.

"It's not you," she said, her head still resting on her hands on the steering wheel. "I just do this sometimes, come apart at the seams. I don't know why. Don't pay any attention to me."

"Are you all right?" he asked her, though even any bonehead could see that she wasn't. Why did people always say that in situations when clearly everything was not all right? Probably because, like him, they didn't have a clue about what was happening, or what to do about it.

"Oh, sure," she said, raising her head. "I'll be fine." She sat up, and he had to remove his hand before it got caught between her and the seat back. She dragged the back of her hand across her eyes. "I must look a wreck."

He thought she looked beautiful. Her cheeks were flushed, her eyes were bright and sparkly with tears, and her mouth looked soft and—but this didn't seem the right time to be thinking like that. Not when she was upset and vulnerable. They were friends, that was all. The last thing he needed right now was another complication in his life.

"You look okay to me." He couldn't stop himself from hooking a strand of her hair back over her ear.

"I'm really mortified," she said. "Just forget this ever happened."

"Okay," he said, not really sure what *had* happened.

She gave herself a shake. "Okay, then. Let's go see how Dad and Jeremy are doing. I bet they're right where we left them."

They were. Jeremy had pulled a chair next to Dr. Roper's, and he had a pair of pliers in his hand. Naturally, they hadn't heard Ivy and Theo come in, so they didn't look up, but were bent intently over something while Dr. Roper signed one-handed to Jeremy because he held tweezers in the other hand, completing some delicate operation. When it was done, they high-fived each other before noticing Ivy and Theo standing in the doorway.

Jeremy signed, **Come see this, Theo. We put a pilot in the cockpit. He's got goggles and a hat and even a mustache.**

It was pretty neat, Theo had to admit. The little pilot looked almost alive, ready to take on the Red Baron and then go find some admiring mademoiselle in a smoky café.

Pretty cool. You ready to go home now?

Jeremy threw a quick, desperate look at Dr. Roper.

He can stay awhile, if that's okay, Dr. Roper signed.

Jeremy's anxious glance moved back to Theo, his eyes pleading.

Oh, I guess it's okay. We don't have to go right away.

Thank you, thank you, thank you, Jeremy signed, and turned directly back to the airplane in front of him. Dr. Roper did, too.

"Well, okay," Ivy said, back in the hall. "We've lost them. So you can stay here or you can go with me to Harry's and to Hazel's. I need to deliver their dinners and give them another signing lesson."

"They're still at it?"

"Oh, yeah. They're really serious. They bought some signing videos and a dictionary. They're getting pretty good, too. I spend some time helping them when I make my deliveries."

"Huh," he said, dumbfounded. Somebody who didn't have to was actually committed to learning to sign. He didn't get it. "Well, okay, I guess I'll go with you. I'd like to see this."

9

Harry and Hazel were signing in the equivalent of baby talk—slow and awkward and simple, but they were able to communicate in a very basic way. And they were thrilled to be able to do it.

"Ivy, I want you to teach me to sign that Harry's an old poophead," Hazel said.

"Oh, come on, Hazel," Ivy said. "Wouldn't you like to learn something more—oh, I don't know—dignified?"

"I want to learn stuff that I'll actually use in my real life. Isn't that what communication's about, being able to say what you want to?"

"Yeah, okay you're right. Well, let's see—poophead . . ." Ivy pondered and then experimented with a sign that made Theo laugh. "How's that look to you?" she asked him.

"Does the job," he said, still laughing.

"Okay, so watch this, Hazel. Here's *Harry is a poophead.*" Hazel carefully imitated her.

"Lucky for you I'm too much of a gentleman to learn something I could answer you with," Harry said. "But I want a word with Ivy in private before she leaves."

"Got it, Harry," Ivy said. "For one of those answers you're too much of a gentleman to use, right?"

Harry pressed his lips together, suppressing a smile, and signed, **I'm not talking**.

Before Theo knew it, almost an hour had gone by as he watched Ivy teach Harry and Hazel to sign. They clearly thought it was the next best thing to a miracle, which made him feel ill tempered and cross for not participating. But he couldn't make himself lift his hands to do so.

Ivy seemed to have recovered from her outburst of earlier in the afternoon. She was signing away with Harry and Hazel as if she had nothing more on her mind than making sure they got the difference between *fall* and *ax*.

Suddenly she looked at her watch and signed, **Time to go**. "It's getting late," she added, "and Theo's got to collect his little brother."

"You've got a little brother?" Harry asked. "Can he sign, too?"

"Well, sure," Theo said. "He's deaf."

"You don't say," Harry said, sounding surprised. "I don't know why, but I was thinking, if you had brothers and sisters they'd be like you—able to hear."

"Nope. My mom was born deaf, but not my dad, so the

genetics are complicated. I'm the only one in my family who can hear."

"Well, how do you like that," Harry said. "I never knew of such a thing."

With that, Theo felt like a freak all over again—and, as he often did, guilty for feeling resentful toward his family when he was the one lucky enough to hear.

The ride home on Theo's bike was silent, of course, because Jeremy had his arms around Theo's middle. But as soon as he jumped off at home, he was signing rapidly.

That was so fun. Those planes are the neatest things. I want Dad to see them. He likes to build things. I bet he could really get into it.

At dinner—canned soup and cold cuts fixed by Thomas because Palma was too busy working to think about dinner—Jeremy kept on about the airplanes. And Thomas *was* interested. He wanted to go with Jeremy next time, to see them, if that would be okay with Dr. Roper.

Theo watched him eat spoonfuls of cream of mushroom soup and slices of cheese and salami—all things that probably weren't good for somebody with high blood pressure and high cholesterol—and wished he could become one of Ivy's clients and have a delicious healthy dinner waiting for them all every evening.

Well, why couldn't they become clients? Palma could certainly afford it, and it would relieve Thomas of the last-minute evening scramble of coming up with something edible for them all. Besides, he already practically had an investment in her business, considering how much time he spent helping out and delivering stuff. He sat marshaling his arguments for Palma, while Jeremy and Thomas ate and Palma took tiny sips of her soup, ignored the cold cuts, and cocked her head the way she did when she was listening only to her own thoughts.

I want to go back tomorrow, Jeremy signed. **Can I, Theo? Can I go back when you do? I know that's where you've been going almost every afternoon. I won't be any trouble. And then Dad can stop by on the way home from work and see the models.**

I'll have to check it out with Ivy and make sure her dad's going to be there, and if it's okay if you two come by. I'll call her right after dinner.

Palma suddenly rose, the napkin in her lap falling to the floor unnoticed, and headed back to the studio without a word.

The Posse looked at each other, shrugged, and resumed eating. That was Palma for you—tuned only to her own frequency.

When Theo spoke to Ivy after dinner, she said her father would be home the next afternoon and he was enthusiastic about having both Jeremy and Thomas come over to see his models. She said that though he belonged to a model airplane club, he didn't go often because communication was a problem. The prospect of sharing his hobby and his passion with a couple of guys who spoke his language was too good to pass up.

Theo exhaled with relief when he hung up to know that he wouldn't be abandoning Jeremy to too much TV and too many computer games for yet another afternoon.

The next night at dinner, over some of Ivy's pork loin with mustard sauce and spinach-stuffed tomatoes—a sample to help sell Palma on becoming a client—the talk, after some initial astonishment at the wonderful dinner, was all about model airplanes. Palma surfaced long enough from her creative preoccupation to be appreciative of the food, if not of the airplane talk.

So what do you think? Theo asked her. Wouldn't you like to eat like this four nights a week?

What would it cost? Palma asked.

Theo told her.

Would she give us a discount?

Why? Theo asked. It's already reasonable.

Well, does she know who I am?

Theo raised his hands but then couldn't think what to say. What difference does it make who you are? Or: you can afford it better than most of her customers? Or: for Pete's sake, just say yes. What's the big deal?

Palma waited for him to sign something as she watched Jeremy and Thomas eat. Then, before Theo could answer, she smiled and signed, **All right. I like to see my men eat so well.**

Since when? Theo thought, but he wasn't going to mess up the deal by getting smart. Who knew what whims moved Palma. He would like to think she realized how petty and cheap she sounded, but that probably wasn't it. **Great,** he signed. **I'll make the arrangements.**

Palma rose, still beaming down on them benevolently. Maybe there was something about sharing a wonderful meal that made her act that way.

I'll be in the studio, she said, and wafted off through the kitchen. Theo heard the back door slam.

Pop and I are going to fly with Dr. Roper on Saturday, Jeremy signed to Theo. **He said we could help him, but I'm scared to. What if I crash one?**

He wouldn't have invited you if he didn't want you, Thomas signed.

Theo could tell Thomas was excited, too. Although Thomas went to the Deaf Club meetings and outings, it wasn't often that he got together with one other man just to do guy things. Theo knew he must feel isolated at work, where he was the only deaf person. And though furniture-making, which wasn't just his job but a source of real pleasure, was a fairly solitary activity, it couldn't have been pleasant for him to feel so completely apart.

. . .

The next week, Ben Roper was doing business from home because his office was being painted, so Jeremy was able to spend every afternoon working on the airplanes with him. Thomas joined them after work on three of those afternoons. He and Ben Roper enjoyed each other's company, and Jeremy was elated to be able to spend so much time with men who treated him like one of them—and to have an activity that was so totally consuming and fascinating to him. Although Thomas and Jeremy were spending hours together at something Theo wasn't the slightest bit interested in, he didn't feel left out at all. With them occupied, and Palma lost in her current projects, he was free to work on the computer, to play his pickup basketball games—and to hang around Ivy's kitchen, not to mention having time to be her meal-toting vassal.

On their way home after an afternoon of meal deliveries and another signing lesson for Hazel and Harry, Ivy said, "They're getting good, aren't they? I never thought they'd stick with it."

"It's you," Theo said. "You're a natural teacher. They love you."

She looked over at him. "Yeah?"

"Yeah."

"Well, don't stop now. Tell me some more."

"What more is there? You *are* a natural teacher. They *do* love you."

"We've been spending hours together every week, you've

been eating my food like it's all that's keeping you alive, and that's the best you can do?"

What did she mean? What was he supposed to say? Thank you? I like the purple stripe in your hair? You're a great cook? What? She was making him feel guilty and he wasn't even sure why. What *was* it with women? Between Ivy and Palma, he was going nuts. Give him a nice, uncomplicated mathematical problem any day, or a basketball game with a bunch of guys who didn't communicate except with grunts.

"Uh—" he began.

"Oh, never mind," she snapped. "If I have to pry it out of you, it's not worth it."

In silence, she drove to his house and stopped at the curb, the motor running.

"But Jeremy's at your house," Theo said. "I was supposed to bring him home."

"He can ride your bike home. I'll send dinner with him. Why don't you just get out now."

He wanted to ask what he'd done, but he had a feeling it wouldn't do any good. She was in another one of those odd moods of hers, and all he really wanted was to get away from it.

"Fine," he said, and got out, slamming the door.

Palma was in the studio after dinner and the Posse was watching TV when the doorbell rang. Jeremy and Thomas ignored the flashing light, so Theo went to answer the door.

Ivy stood there, a paper sack in her hand. She held it out to him. "Peace offering?"

He hesitated, but took it.

"Will you come outside and take a walk with me?" Ivy asked.

Again he hesitated.

"Please. I need to tell you something."

"Okay. Let me get my jacket."

They went down the three steps to the sidewalk, hands in pockets, shoulders hunched against the chill evening. Chimney smoke showed in gray smudges against the black sky, and its scent perfumed the autumn night.

For once, Theo knew enough to keep quiet, to wait for her to start.

"You know those—outbursts, I guess you could call them—that I have from time to time?"

As if he could have missed noticing them. "Yeah."

"Well, there's a reason for them. I'm not always tuned in to it myself when I'm having them, but I usually figure it out later. I just wanted you to know, it doesn't have anything to do with you. Not really."

"Yeah?" He didn't seem to know what else to say.

"I think one of the reasons I have them around you is because I feel safe with you. I know you won't—well, I don't know what. But I know they bother you. How could they not? They bother *me*."

"Okay," he said. That seemed innocuous enough. He had to admit he was curious. And he also had to admit that he liked how willing she was to tell him things, to keep letting him in on what was happening inside her. So different from Palma, who just flipped up and down as if it were normal behavior and needed no explanation. Ivy at least knew it wasn't. And he liked that she felt safe with him—especially when he didn't always feel safe with himself.

"It's about my mother," Ivy said.

"I thought she was long gone. Do you still talk to her?"

"She *is* long gone. And no, I don't talk to her. But her shadow hangs around. I guess it always will."

"Hmmm," he said. Were they talking about ghosts here?

"You think you have problems with *your* mother, but what if you didn't even have a mother?"

"Sounds okay to me." He thought about what it would be like to come home to quiet every day, to regular meals and freedom and people who were taking care of their own business.

"That's what you think," Ivy said. "What do you think it feels like to know you weren't good enough to make her want to stay? That she was willing to go off somewhere by herself rather than be with you?"

"Hey," he said, "the people who run off are the ones with

the problem. Not the people they leave behind. What your mother did doesn't have anything to do with you."

"How can you know that? Look how much you like to get away from Jeremy, and all he wants is some conversation and help with his homework. I was younger. I needed a lot more than that a lot more of the time. I needed too much. I drove her away."

But weren't parents supposed to like taking care of little kids, even if it was hard? If they didn't, why did they *have* kids, anyway? He wondered who had done it all for him when he was a baby. He had a hard time imagining Palma as the perfect doting mommy. Had it always been all Thomas?

"That's still not a good reason to take off," he said. "Kids grow up. It gets easier. You love them anyway. Besides, someday they'll have to help you dress and feed yourself, so you can get even."

She stopped at the corner in front of the Congregational Church and sat down on the steps. She shivered at the feel of the cold stone through her jeans. Theo stood in front of her, one foot on the step beside her, his hands balled up in his pockets.

"All I'm trying to tell you is that sometimes I get sad about her leaving. And I wonder if I was why she left. Just one more thing too much when she was already married to a deaf guy, which is hard enough."

"Maybe the deaf guy is why she left, not you."

"Then why didn't she take me with her?"

"Would you have wanted that? To leave your dad? He's such a cool guy. And he likes having you around."

"I want her to have wanted me. I want her to think about me now."

"How do you know she doesn't?" He couldn't say why he was enjoying this, because it was like trying to pull an elephant uphill when it didn't want to go, but he didn't want her to feel responsible for some obvious flake's irresponsible decision to take off when the going got even a little bit tough.

"Because"—she held up her fingers and began counting on them—"one, she never calls; two, she never writes; three, she never remembers my birthday or Christmas; and four, she never even said goodbye. She did the worst thing anybody's ever done to me: she just disappeared."

"Oh." Then, "Maybe she met with foul play. Maybe she *can't* call or write." He was on the verge of suggesting they call the cops. Ivy's mother could be lying in a shallow grave somewhere, a devoted wife and mother unjustly accused of desertion.

She made a face at him. "Only if kidnappers made her file for divorce at gunpoint and insist that her attorney handle any communication with us because she didn't want to be bothered."

"Oh. Well, I still think she's the one with the problem. That just makes me surer. Nobody with all their marbles could refuse to have anything to do with you." There. He'd said it, let out what he thought about her. His heart was boogying in his chest.

She raised her head and looked at him. "Yeah?"

"Yeah." He kept looking at her and she didn't look away. He understood now how much she feared someone's not appreciating her, and how she was willing to push someone away if she suspected lack of interest, before she was the one being left. She was afraid, not irrational, and that made it easier for him to accept her moods.

She stood and dusted the seat of her jeans. "Well, what do you know anyway," she said. But when she lowered her head, he saw, in the light over the church door, a smile tug at the corners of her mouth. "We should go. It's cold and dark out here."

"Need I remind you, this walk was your idea. Cold and dark was just fine with you not so long ago."

"Don't you know better than to expect a female to be consistent?" she asked, tucking her hand into the pocket of his jacket.

"What happened to women wanting to be equal to men?" he asked, putting his hand over hers inside his pocket.

"Equal," she said. "It doesn't mean exactly the same." Against his palm, she finger-spelled Hi.

Hi, too, he finger-spelled into hers.

They walked back to Theo's hand in hand, breathing in

the crisp cold air, feeling warmer than their jackets were making them. All he said on the way was, "So what did you bring me in that bag?"

And she answered, a bit smugly, "Meringue chocolate-chip kisses."

Lying in bed that night, Theo considered the logic of unmothered Ivy using her culinary skills to nurture almost everybody in her life. He wondered if she recognized how motherly that was. And thinking about that made him wonder how he might also be manifesting things that went on in his family without even knowing it.

10

The first Saturday afternoon in October he was at the Coopers' with Ivy, being the brawn to her brains as he hauled bowls of salad, pans of corn bread, platters of ham and turkey, and, with great trepidation, the enormous double-chocolate fudge cake into their small kitchen. Somehow Ivy had found a place for everything and was helping the sisters set up tables and chairs in the sunroom at the back of the house.

"Hurry, Rochelle," Adele said. "They'll be coming in about twenty minutes."

"Oh, cool off," Rochelle said. "You know nobody in our family has been on time for anything except church in their whole lives, and they're not about to start a good habit now. We got plenty of time."

Theo watched them, knowing they were doing something he could never do with his only sibling; he'd never be able to banter with Jeremy while they were both doing something that involved the use of their hands. There was a degree of spontaneity that he and Jeremy would never have if they had to wait until their hands were free to say what had popped into their minds.

Rochelle was right: it was an hour before the first party guest arrived, and by that time the arrangements were complete. Adele and Rochelle, dressed alike in white dresses similar to the ones they wore in the photograph on the mantel, were giving themselves a wingding of a party. Balloons and streamers, music and laughter, ear-splitting shrieks of pleasure over opened presents—it was the kind of event Theo had never seen. Deaf Club parties and family birthday celebrations were completely silent events with everyone watching each other intently to keep up with the fast and furious signing. All at the party was not purely harmonious, though—and not just between the children, whose squabbles didn't seem to affect their willingness to keep playing together. He saw what he thought were the same two women from the photograph in the living room going at each other in the same way—blazing eyes and pointed fingers. And he saw two old men arguing endlessly and circularly about whose favorite football team had the best chance of winning the championship. But here they all were, in the same house, celebrating the same occasion, a family in spite of all that.

You think the twins are on a sugar high? Ivy signed to Theo as they listened to Adele's rapid-fire laugh.

How could they not be, after that cake? Theo signed back.

"You two talking about us?" Adele said, catching them at it. "What's this mean?" She imitated the sign for *cake.*

Ivy made it again. "It means 'cake,' that's all. We just like seeing you have such a good time."

"Well, we're definitely having one," she said. "Why shouldn't we? You got to grab your moments and squeeze them dry. Enjoy them while you're having them. Then remember them and enjoy them all over again in your memory. And try to have more good ones than bad ones—or at least remember more of the good ones."

"You're a philosopher," Ivy told her.

"Oh, no," Adele said. "I just pay attention to what life's got to tell me. Now, here I am loaded with all this experience and all this knowledge and hardly anybody wants to hear about it. So I decided I just don't care if they want it or not—they're going to get it. Someday they'll think back, probably when I'm not around anymore to gloat, and say, Oh, so that's what she meant." She gave out with her machine-gun laugh again. "So you pay attention."

Theo saluted her and clicked his heels together. Ivy imitated him as Adele drifted off to her party.

"Think she's got a point?" Theo asked.

"Someday we'll know, I guess. But you can't gloat."

"No danger from me. Gloating's not my specialty." He

paused and then went on. "If you're not doing anything after the party, I could show you what is."

Now where did *that* come from? He was as surprised by himself as Ivy looked. He had no experience with flirtatious behavior and, as far as he knew, hadn't a clue about how to do it—but that's what it sounded as if he was doing. And what did he mean by that anyway? The only specialty he could show her was some fancy calculus equations. Or maybe he could explain elementary fluid dynamics.

"Could you be clearer about that?" Ivy asked. She was smiling in a way he hadn't seen her smile before.

He made the sign for *connection*, the thumb and index finger of one hand linked in a circle through the same circle made by the other hand. Palma had once made that sign into a silver sculpture that he liked better than anything else she had ever done. It seemed perfectly to express the idea of closeness to another being in heart and mind, with the expectation of a future, and of a continued growing together. He'd been surprised that Palma understood such a feeling, and had been surprised, too, at himself and how much he wanted that feeling for himself.

"With me?" she asked, her eyebrows way up.

"I think I've been waiting for you for a long time. Before I even knew you." Where were these smooth words coming from? He'd always thought he was less articulate with his voice than with his hands, because it seemed that he used his hands so much more. But with Ivy, who spoke both his languages, who switched back and forth in them the way he did, who valued them both maybe even more than he did, he could be articulate in both.

"Well, my goodness, Theo." She flushed and looked down—but then looked up quickly, right into his eyes. They stood, their hands an inch apart on the kitchen counter, just looking at each other.

"Oh, honey," Rochelle said, coming upon them. "What's going on here? I thought you two were just business associates, and now look at this."

They turned to her, both a little guilty, a little annoyed at the interruption, a little relieved.

"Well, don't let me interfere with this whatever-it-is," Rochelle went on. "I had my share of beaux in my time, so I know how it is. I just never did find the one I could stand being with for the long haul, but that doesn't mean it can't happen. I came in to get some more ice, but ice isn't what's going on here, I can see that." She teeheed some while she filled the ice bucket, and then went out, letting the swinging door close behind her.

What had been easy and natural between Theo and Ivy now took on an awkward shade. Until Ivy smiled at him, a soft, affectionate smile. "Where were we?" she said. "Oh, yes. Well, after the party, I'm completely free. All we have to do is clean up. Then we're on our own. Aren't we?"

"Completely," Theo said. "Dad and Jeremy are with your

father doing airplane things. Palma's working. I have no obligations." For once in my life, he thought, I'm free at exactly the right time.

The phone on the wall in the kitchen rang, making them both jump. On the fourth ring, Ivy said, "I guess it's too noisy at the party for them to hear." She picked it up. "Hello. Yes," she said. "This is she."

That's odd, Theo thought. Who would be calling Ivy here?

Her eyes darted in his direction and then away. "Yes," she said again. "I'll put him on." She held the phone out to him, her face stiff, her hand trembling. "It's the relay operator. It's my father calling you."

Theo took the phone, but he already knew it was bad. Using a relay operator was such a hassle for a deaf person that they avoided it except when absolutely necessary.

"Hello," Theo said, surprised that he was able to keep his voice steady.

"This is the relay operator." Her voice was so loud, the way some of them thought they had to speak, even to the party without the hearing loss, that he knew Ivy could hear every word she said. She spoke exactly what she read off the TTY from Ivy's father. "This call is from Dr. Ben Roper. Your father was taken ill at my house and has gone by ambulance to Mercy Hospital. I've called your mother, and she's on her way to the hospital. I have Jeremy with me. Don't worry about him."

"I'm on my way to the hospital, too. What happened?" He waited while the operator typed the questions for transmittal to Dr. Roper's TTY, then waited some more for Dr. Roper to type his answer.

"I'm not sure. He just collapsed. Maybe a stroke. I'll keep Jeremy with me for as long as necessary."

"Thank you. I'll be in touch. Tell Jeremy not to worry." He didn't know how he could even say such a thing. He handed the phone back to Ivy.

"Do you want me to drive you?" she asked.

"How can you? You have to finish with the party." He was dazed, unbelieving. How was something like this possible? A minute ago, everything had been completely normal, better than normal even, on the edge of something wonderful. And suddenly nothing in his life was the same as it had been. And he had the bleak feeling that it would be a long time, if ever, before things felt normal again.

Ivy pulled the car keys from her jeans pocket. "Here. Take the car. Bring it back whenever you can. I can walk home from here. Call me. No matter what time it is. And don't worry about Jeremy. We'll take care of him."

Numbly, he took the keys. "Thanks."

He sat in the car, the keys in the ignition but not turned on. He wanted to savor these last few moments of ignorance before he knew how all their lives might have changed. Then, sighing, he started the car and drove to the hospital.

11

Before he even got to the ICU, he could hear Palma. He knew it was her even though he had heard her voice so rarely. It had the hollow, guttural quality of a person to whom sound was a mystery, a sensation rather than a sense. He increased his pace until he was almost running, knowing how frightened she would be, and how frustrated at not being able to communicate it. In the world of the hearing, aside from those who knew her art, without her interpreters and protectors, she was as helpless and desperate as an infant, not the star she regarded herself but simply a mute and terrified woman.

When she saw him she rushed to him, her hands flying. **I can't find out—they won't let me see him—they have no interpreter—they say one's on the way—where have you been?**

For the first time in his life, he did to another person what he had always hated having done to him—he took her hands in his and held them. Her eyes blazed at him, and a long, low sound came from her. Then she closed her eyes and leaned her head against his shoulder. She, who had always seemed so large and formidable, he now realized, was a small, almost fragile woman.

"I'm her son," he said to the cluster of hospital personnel around them. "I can interpret if somebody will just tell me what's going on."

"Thank God," said a man in a white coat with COCHRAN embroidered in blue on the breast pocket. "I'm Dr. Cochran. I admitted your father. I'm afraid I didn't know he was deaf. Now that I understand that—well, it changes things."

"How could you not know he was deaf?" Theo asked, outraged at the unknown terrors and humiliations his father might have suffered as a result of this oversight.

"Well," Dr. Cochran said, somewhat huffily, "after a stroke, trouble with speech is not uncommon. Nor is difficulty in understanding what is said."

"What about the ambulance attendants? Didn't they know? They picked him up at another deaf man's house, for God's sake—a man who had to use an interpreter even to complete an emergency call." Theo felt himself growing large with fury.

"Things are often confused during an emergency," Dr. Cochran went on in a mollifying voice. "We try to act as fast as we can to treat the condition. There isn't always time for a full history."

"He couldn't have given you *any* history." Theo's voice was loud and strident, and he realized his grip on Palma was so tight he was probably hurting her. But she didn't complain. She simply leaned against him, her eyes closed, leaving all the messy, difficult stuff to him. A surge of resentment and inadequacy rose in him even as he knew that she couldn't have done any good by herself anyway. After all, she'd tried; he'd heard her all the way down the hall.

"Well, now that you're here," Cochran said, "let's see if we can get some things clear. I need the name of his doctor; age; occupation; insurance information; recent complaints, all that. I understand that you're upset, but—"

A nurse came hurrying up, whispered in his ear, and then hurried away again. Theo figured she was used to scenes of high drama in the hospital and could ignore theirs—but it was the first such scene Theo had ever been involved in, and every moment of it seemed to vibrate with alarm.

"Ah," Cochran said, "the interpreter is here. Perhaps he can deal with your mother while I have a talk with you."

"I want to see my father," Theo said firmly. "And so does my mother. We want to do that first, before anything else. And my mother can understand anything you want to talk to me about. She doesn't need anybody to *deal* with her."

He didn't know where this sense of command was coming from, but suddenly he knew what he wanted and that he wasn't going to let some guy in a white coat keep him from getting to Thomas. Just because Cochran had spent a lot of years and a lot of dollars getting his medical education didn't mean he could boss them around. Thomas was his father, for God's sake, and he was alone and sick and probably scared if he was able to feel anything at all. Keeping them away from him qualified as cruelty.

"Well, he's being worked on," Cochran began.

"I don't care," Theo said. "We want to see him. No one even seems to know what's really wrong with him, especially since you haven't been able to communicate with him."

Cochran was silent for a moment and then said, "Okay. Follow me." He led them down a corridor and into an area where a nurse sat at a console with rooms branching out around her like the spokes of a wheel so she could keep an eye on several patients at once. "Where's Mr. . . . ?" He looked up at Theo.

"Dennison," Theo told him.

"Mr. Dennison," Dr. Cochran told her. "This is his son and his wife. They need to see him."

"Well, I'm not sure," the nurse began. "He's only just—"

"They need to see him," Dr. Cochran repeated. "Now."

"Number four," the nurse said, getting the message.

Theo and Palma went to stand at the foot of Thomas's

bed. He was surrounded by a clutter of paraphernalia on both sides, with tubes going into both arms, oxygen into his nose, and another tube or two disappearing under the sheets.

"Because of his apparent language difficulties," Dr. Cochran said, "we assumed a stroke. His blood pressure seemed to substantiate this, as well as the headache he indicated he was having. In spite of the mix-up about the deafness, I believe the diagnosis will still be confirmed. Do you want to try to communicate with him? That can help us know how significant the damage is."

Damage, thought Theo. Significant damage.

"There does appear to be considerable weakness on the left side."

"Weakness?" Theo asked. "Does that mean paralysis?"

"Well, to some extent. Yes."

Would Thomas still be able to sign?

What's he saying? What's he saying? Palma kept asking. But Theo was too busy and preoccupied to answer her right away.

Working his way around the medical equipment, Theo went to Thomas's side and touched his face. His father's eyes remained closed. Theo took Thomas's right hand and finger-spelled **T-h-e-o** into it. There was no reaction.

At that point, Theo told a frantic Palma as much as he knew about what was going on. He asked her to stay with Thomas, to hold his hand and to sign into it, just so he'd know he wasn't alone, so he'd know there was someone with him who spoke his language. While she did that, Theo would try to get the full scoop from the doctors.

No matter what Palma said, or Thomas, or anybody in the Deaf Club, about how normally they lived their lives, about how they didn't need to be fixed or changed, or to have cochlear implants, about how interesting and rich the culture of the deaf was, there were times when it wasn't the least bit normal or rich or interesting—when being deaf was a plain catastrophe. And this was one of them.

Thomas really shouldn't be left without someone who could both speak and sign for a single minute. What if he woke up and needed something? Or was having a pain or a symptom that he couldn't tell anybody about? What if he needed comfort, or information, or company? Hearing patients could use anybody who happened by—a nurse, a candy striper, a janitor—to fill these roles. But Thomas— who was Thomas to use?

Dr. Cochran was moderately reassuring. Thomas had passed through the critical first few hours. Because they'd assumed he was having a stroke, and because that apparently was what he actually had had, he'd received the appropriate treatment. It was early yet to evaluate the extent of his problems, but that would come in time. All they could do now was wait and watch.

"I'll stay with him," Theo said. "If he wakes up, he'll need somebody he can talk to."

"We have the interpreter here now," Dr. Cochran said. "And we can get someone when the need arises."

"He'll be more comfortable with me," Theo said. "I'm staying."

"If you insist." Dr. Cochran didn't sound happy about it, but at least he wasn't giving Theo an argument.

Only later, in the wakeful hours of the night, did Theo consider the doctor's point of view—how difficult and frustrating and even annoying it would be to try to treat a person he couldn't communicate with, whether his native language was Russian or Thai or sign. In the half-light from various monitors and machines and night-lights, Theo made the sign of connection that he had made what now seemed weeks ago, to Ivy in the Cooper sisters' kitchen. How important that link was. How vital. How fragile.

It was then he realized he hadn't called her. He'd sent Palma off to pick Jeremy up at the Ropers'. Even though she didn't like to drive—any diva worth her salt preferred to be chauffeured—this was one day, and maybe one month or year or even lifetime, when it wasn't going to be all about Palma anymore. She was going to have to come down to earth and see to the running of the house and the care of Jeremy in a way she hadn't done for a long time. If she ever had. They were all going to have to recognize how much of the family load Thomas had carried, and to take some of it on for themselves. And one thing Theo was sure about was that nobody was going to like it.

He left Thomas for long enough to call Ivy. Her voice, when she answered, was foggy with sleep.

"God, I'm sorry," Theo said. "But you said call anytime, and I only just got myself straightened out enough to do it. I've been too wired to think about sleep, so I guess I forgot other people have gone to bed by now."

"It's okay, don't worry about it." She cleared her throat. "Anyway, the phone won't wake Dad up, you know. Your mother's pretty upset. I couldn't get much from her. How's your father?"

"It's hard to tell. He's still mostly out of it, but the doctor is, as they say, guardedly optimistic. I just don't want him to wake up and be alone, with no way to tell anybody what he needs."

"Well, of course you don't. Your mother's coming back to the hospital first thing in the morning, after she drops Jeremy off here. They stayed for supper, but I don't think anybody was paying much attention to what we ate."

"How's Jeremy?"

"Upset. Bewildered. Scared to death. My dad's upset, too. He's awfully fond of Thomas."

They listened to the hum of the phone wires for a long moment. Then Ivy said, "If there's anything—and I really mean anything—I can do, just ask me. I can't guess what you need or I'd do it without waiting to be asked."

"I know. Jeremy, I guess. Watch out for him. I don't know when I'll be able to leave here, and I know he's worried. I'll get him in to see Pop as soon as I can. Your car's still here, too. In the front parking lot."

"Don't worry about it. My dad can bring me over to pick it up. I don't suppose they'd let me come sit with you."

"Family only, that's the rule for ICU. Maybe later."

"Okay. Call me if there's any news."

"Sure. Be prepared to see Palma at 5 a.m. If I know her, she'll be awake all night, drinking coffee and throwing things around in her studio."

"Why shouldn't she be? She's as scared and upset as anybody. The only reason she's not *there* drinking coffee is because of Jeremy. We offered to let him stay overnight here, but she thought he should have a parent with him right now. So don't be too hard on her."

"I know, I know. You're right. I'm just—"

"I know you are. I'll take some food by your house tomorrow so you'll all have something to eat whenever you get home."

"Thanks. Mrs. Chang next door has a key. I'll tell her to expect you. You've been—well, how can I tell you—"

"Never mind. Just get your dad better and bring him home."

12

After he hung up, he thought about Palma. She'd grasped the need to be with Jeremy rather than at the hospital, where she must have wanted more to be. But she'd known Theo would have had to be there, too, to interpret for her, and then Jeremy would have been without either of them. Maybe she wasn't as selfish and self-involved as he'd always thought. And maybe prima donnas only got to be that way because other people let them get away with it.

He must have dozed because the room was bright when he opened his eyes. And Palma was there, along with Dr. Cochran.

Is he okay? Palma signed. **Tell me what the doctor's saying.**

Okay, okay. Wait a minute. Let me wake up. He stood and stretched, looking over at Thomas as he did so. Somehow he didn't appear as sick as he had last night. He was still asleep, but his color was better and he seemed, in a way Theo couldn't explain, more like himself.

"Good morning, Theo," Dr. Cochran said. "Good news this morning. We're sure now it was an ischemic event, not a hemorrhagic one, and we got the thrombolytic agents started in time, so the damage will be dramatically minimized."

"Hold it a second. I need some translations here."

While the doctor explained the technicalities of Thomas's diagnosis and treatment, Theo translated as well as he could for Palma, who kept interrupting. Theo had to wave her off and keep going to keep up with Dr. Cochran.

When he was finished, they all looked over at Thomas. His eyes were open and his hands were trying to sign, in spite of the IVs in his arms and the obvious weakness and lack of control in his left side.

Palma threw herself across him, sobbing in a loud and harsh voice, unable to hear the doctor squawking about the disturbance to the monitors, the patient, the bedclothes, and several other things. Thomas patted her awkwardly with his one good hand, and tried to smile with half his mouth.

Theo felt tears in his own eyes. Since he couldn't get anywhere near Thomas himself, he had to be satisfied with watching his parents. He was embarrassed to admit that as debilitated as Thomas clearly was, Theo felt a welling of relief at his evidence of competence. Theo needed him to be his father again, to help him feel not so alone and inadequate.

Hi, Pop, he signed.

Thomas needed two hands to sign **What's happening?** but only one hand was working properly. Still, Theo was able to figure out what his father was asking. He answered as well as he could, trying to keep it simple, knowing that Thomas was ill, and tired, and was surely being distracted by Palma wallowing on top of him. Lucky for him he couldn't hear all her carrying-on.

The whole time Theo was signing to his father, he was thinking, What will happen if Pop can use only one hand? How will he express himself? How will he work? What about his magic?

"His hand," Theo said to the doctor. "What will happen with it? Will he be able to use it again?"

"That's part of the stroke sequelae. My guess is that he'll slowly regain the use of it, though he may always be somewhat weaker on his left side than his right."

"Don't you know how important it is for him to be able to use both his hands?" Theo heard the desperation in his own voice, and the anger, but he couldn't help himself. "They're his means of communication, of making a living, of entertaining himself. You have to give him back his hands."

The doctor frowned and opened his mouth to speak, then closed it again. Taking a deep breath, he said, "Certainly I know how important his hands are. And we're doing everything we can to make sure he has the use of them for everything he wants to do. But we're only doctors, not wizards. And the family will need to have a part in his recovery, too. He'll have to have help with his therapy, with his diet, his exercise, his stress levels. You can all help him with that."

"We will," Theo promised, ashamed of his weakness and of his fear. "We'll do everything. When can he come home?" Nothing seemed more important than getting Thomas out of there and back to where he could be himself again. The way he used to be.

"We'll have to see how he does. A week probably. And he'll still need lots of therapy."

Two of the ICU nurses had managed to pry Palma off Thomas's bed and had given her a chair so she could sit beside him signing madly, asking questions, telling him how worried she'd been. Thomas lay back on his pillow, his face turned to her with a look of confusion on it.

Theo tapped Palma's shoulder, and she shot him an irritated glance, her hands stopped in midair.

Slow down. He's tired and confused. He can't keep up with you.

Palma looked at Thomas, who nodded slowly, and back

at Theo. She lowered her hands to her lap and bent her head over them, the picture of remorse.

Oh, please, Theo thought. This is not the time for your dramatics. He tapped her again. **Just go slow.**

She raised her hands in the gesture of a maestro about to play the piano, and slowly signed, **How do you feel?**

With effort, Thomas brought his left hand to his stomach and rested his right middle finger on his forehead, the sign for *sick*. Then he struck his chest several times in the sign for *happy* and moved both hands, the right better than the left, upward in the sign for *alive*.

I'm happy you're alive, too, she signed.

Ditto, Theo signed.

"Okay, let's let him sleep now," Dr. Cochran said. "You can come back later. Why don't you go home and get some rest?"

There was nothing Theo wanted to do more, though he felt guilty for even thinking of it. But he allowed himself to be propelled out of the room with Palma on his heels signing, **But I want to stay. I just got here.**

You can stay. You can go back in and sit with him while he sleeps. But I have to go home and crash. I've been up almost all night.

You were asleep when I got here. You can't leave me. I need interpreting.

I'll ask the nurse to call an interpreter for you. I have to get some rest. Theo could hardly wait to get away from her, from the hospital, from the whole train wreck. He wanted to sleep and wake up and find that it had all been just a terrible dream.

On the way home he kept thinking of everything that he should be doing, that he didn't want to do. He knew he should be with Jeremy, reassuring him. Somebody needed to tell Thomas's boss what had happened, and that somebody would have to be him. He ought to be at the hospital with his mother, helping her. The health insurance had to be checked, to see what should be done about that. And God only knew what important things he was forgetting about. Or didn't know enough to even think of. But he was exhausted and overwhelmed and used up.

And scared to death.

His hands on the steering wheel were wet and shaky, and he hoped he could make it home without an accident. Though suddenly the idea of being in a nice peaceful coma didn't seem like such a bad idea.

He pulled up in front of the house so weak he had to put his head down on the steering wheel. It had been a long time since he'd last eaten, he realized. Maybe that's what he needed—food.

Ivy's food. If he couldn't have Ivy herself.

On the kitchen counter was a bag of muffins, and in the refrigerator was some kind of casserole covered with grated cheese. Thomas probably wouldn't be able to eat that, Theo thought. Wasn't cheese supposed to be bad for somebody who'd had a stroke?

He dug out a hunk of the casserole, plopped it on a plate, and stuck it in the microwave. While he waited, he wolfed a couple of the muffins. They had a cinnamon-sugar crust on the top and were restorative in a way he couldn't have thought possible. They evoked Ivy in their tang and sweetness and nourishment.

After he'd stuffed down the casserole, he fell on his face on his bed and slept for four hours, waking up, heart pounding, to the ring of the telephone. He staggered into the family room, bouncing off the walls in his sleep-drunken haze. He snatched it up. "Yes?"

"Hi. Is this Theo?"

"Yeah?"

"This is Mike Talbot, the American Sign Language interpreter at Mercy Hospital. I'm calling for your mom."

"What's wrong?" He scrubbed his hand over his face, trying to wake up.

"Nothing's really wrong. She just wants to come home now, and she asked me to call you to come get her."

"How's my father?"

"Coming along, as far as I can tell. You need to talk to the doctor for that, though."

Palma wanted him to come get her? She'd had him waked from a sound sleep for that command? Couldn't she ever think of a solution to a problem that didn't involve him?

"Tell her to call a cab." He fought to keep his voice even. "Make sure she's got money to pay for it."

For once in his life, he wasn't going to jump through whatever hoop she held up. He couldn't think of one good reason to—and maybe it was time for her to start doing a few things for herself, even if she didn't want to. He'd been doing plenty of things he didn't want to do for as long as he could remember.

"Right," Mike said.

"Thanks." And he hung up.

Ten minutes later, just as he'd fallen back to sleep, the phone rang again. This time he'd had the presence of mind to bring the cordless one into his bedroom with him so all he had to do was push a button and hold it against his ear, his face still in the pillow, his eyes still closed. "Yeah?" he mumbled.

"Theo? It's Mike again. Your mom doesn't want to take a cab."

"Does she have money?"

"Yeah. She says it's not the money. She wants you."

He wondered if he was too young to have a stroke. From the way it felt like his blood pressure was going, he could believe it was possible.

"Tell her I'm sleeping, Mike. Tell her we'll talk about it when she gets home."

"Okay." He sounded dubious. "But I'm warning you, she's not going to be happy about it."

"So what else is new?" He hung up the phone and slid back to sleep while a tiny slice of his mind stayed awake, waiting for Palma to hit the front door, frothing at the mouth. He had a second of wondering if that's how it was now for Thomas: to be almost completely asleep except for a little piece of him that was wide awake, but that was too small to do much.

It would have been impossible to sleep through Palma's arrival, accompanied as it was with door-slamming and handbag-and-shoe-throwing. She stomped down the hall in her stocking feet and pushed Theo's door open so hard it crashed against the wall—not that she could be bothered by the noise.

He woke with a jump, in spite of the fact that he'd been expecting something like this. Her hands were going even before he sat up.

How could you do that to me? How could you aban-don me when I needed you?

I didn't abandon you. What's wrong with a cab ride home?

I needed you. The finger she jabbed at him was accusatory.

We should go get Jeremy, Theo said, changing the subject. **He needs us now.**

You'll go get Jeremy, but you wouldn't get me. She turned her back on him, a rude and efficient way of ending a signed conversation.

Theo was off the bed and behind her in an instant,

turning her to face him. **Jeremy's eleven years old. He doesn't have a dime in his pockets. He's a scared little boy.**

Well, I'm scared, too, Palma said, and burst into tears.

"So am I," Theo said, sighing in defeat and putting his arms around his mother. But there was no one to hear him.

13

A week later, Thomas was home. He'd made remarkable progress, but still tired quickly and got easily confused. He seemed happy just to sit by a sunny window, a blanket over his knees, watching TV. For a man who'd always been athletic, his immobility, on top of everything else that had changed about him, made him seem a different person to Theo. He had to wonder how Thomas seemed to himself.

Palma alternated between hovering over him and fleeing to her studio. Theo perfectly understood her impulse to escape to a place where things were as they always had been, since it was a luxury he didn't have. Even when he was at school, he was wondering if the physical therapist had shown up, if Thomas was remembering to take his medications, if Jeremy was handling the situation all right, if there were things he, Theo, should be asking the doctor, but that he was too young and ignorant to think of. But nobody'd asked him if he'd rather wait and grow up first.

Having Thomas at home was supposed to make things easier than when he'd been in the hospital and they'd all spent so much time there, but it had only made them more complicated. He had to be helped with meals and bathing and dressing, with his exercises and his entertainment. Theo supposed he should be glad that at least he wouldn't have to worry about helping him with speech therapy.

On top of and underneath everything Theo did all day, he missed Ivy. No longer were his afternoons free enough to spend time with her, and the moments between classes or the brief bus rides weren't enough. He didn't miss his weights or his computer or his pickup basketball games as much as he missed his kitchen time.

One afternoon, when Thomas had been home for a little more than a week, Theo was plain at the end of his rope, desperate for some small normal part of his old life. The physical therapist was there, working on strengthening Thomas's left side. Palma was in one of her attentive spells, sitting close by, watching hard.

I've got to go out for a while, Theo signed. **I'll take Jeremy with me. We'll be back in time for dinner.**

She stood up, alarmed. **I can't be here alone with him. I can't talk to the therapist. You can't go.**

You can write the therapist a note. Sooner or later you'll have to be alone with him. I'm going.

What if something happens? Her hands flew frantically. **How can I get help?**

Use the TTY. Call me at Ivy's if you have to. That's what it's for.

He turned his back on her and went to find Jeremy. He needed to get out of there, too. He'd been cooped up with illness and fear and gloom for long enough. The two of them needed some therapy of their own now. They needed cookies and model airplanes. And Theo needed a nice big dose of Ivy.

"Everything okay?" the therapist asked. "If you don't mind my saying so, your mom looks like she's about to have a stroke of her own any minute."

"Don't pay any attention to her. She tends to be overreactive. She's not happy I'm going out and leaving her alone here."

"Oh, you need to go," the therapist said as she bent Thomas's elbow and made him squeeze hard on a rubber ball. "The caretakers I see sometimes end up sicker than the patients I'm working with. Just all burned out and used up. I'll do fine with your mom. I'm good at pantomime."

"It's not just that. She's afraid to be alone with my dad."

"Oh, my. Well, she's going to have to get over that. There's a lot of time yet that they'll be together, especially after you and the squirt"—she jerked her thumb at Jeremy—"leave home."

"Like that will ever happen," Theo muttered.

"Hey," she said, taking a couple of steps back and tossing

the ball to Thomas, who caught it neatly in his big, long-fingered, healthy right hand.

The therapist shook her head, patted Thomas's left hand, and threw it again. It bounced off the knuckles of Thomas's left hand and rolled under a chair. Theo knelt down to retrieve it. While he groped, the therapist went on, "You better see that you make it happen. Oh, I know there are families that just love living together on into eternity, but if you ask me, there's always something kind of weird going on there—like somebody's afraid to let go, or somebody's afraid of running their own life. I'm not talking about people from other countries, you know. They've got different beliefs and maybe it works better there." She took the ball from Theo and tossed it to Thomas again, who caught it this time. "But for most of us native-born types, it's best if everybody's got their own stuff taken care of, you know what I mean?"

"Sure," Theo said, wondering if he really did. And also wondering how much this person knew about what she was saying.

Palma had been whacking Theo on the shoulder, trying to get his attention. Finally she came to stand in front of him and signed, I forbid you to go.

Oh, come on, Palma, Theo signed, grinning, holding on to his temper. I'll see you later. He took Jeremy by the arm and pulled him out the door.

Didn't you see what she said? Jeremy asked. **She forbid us to go.**

Yeah. Well, what's she going to do to us? Put us in jail? Kill us?

Wow!

Get in Dad's car. It needs to be driven. We're going to see Ivy.

Does she know we're coming?

No.

Shouldn't we call her?

You want to go back in there and make the call?

Shaking his head, Jeremy opened the car door and got in.

When Theo and Jeremy showed up at the back door, Ivy was in the kitchen. The table was covered with ingredients and she stood over a huge mixing bowl.

Hey, you two! Get in here! I've been missing you.

To Theo's surprise, Jeremy put his arms around Ivy's waist and gave her a hug. She hugged him back while Theo wished he could do the same.

Dad's in his workshop, Jeremy, if you want to go keep him company. But first you have to sit down here and tell me how everything's going.

Got any cookies? Jeremy asked.

And here I thought it was me you came to see. But

she shoved stuff on the table out of the way and set the cookie jar down in the space. **Dig in.**

No second invitations necessary for Jeremy. Theo either.

What are you making? Jeremy asked, indicating the many little bowls on the table.

Fruitcakes.

Jeremy made a face.

"Don't you know there are already enough fruitcakes in the world?" Theo asked her. "The original two dozen are still being passed around as gifts, since no one ever has the nerve to actually eat one."

"Well, those aren't my fruitcakes. Mine are blondes, not brunettes, and they don't have any of that plastic fruit in them. They have macadamia nuts and pineapple and coconut pieces. They're divine."

"I'm reserving judgment."

"Reserve all you want. I'll get you in the end."

He gave her a long look. "Yeah?"

"Count on it." She returned the look.

Theo wished Jeremy would go into Dr. Roper's workshop and come out again in about a week.

These are great, Jeremy signed, his mouth full, as usual.

Want some milk? A beer? A martini? Ivy signed.

Jeremy giggled his strange-sounding giggle, but to Theo it was always an endearing sound. **I'll have a beer.**

Fine. Only thing is, around here, it's white and comes in a carton. That kind okay with you?

That's the only kind I like.

She poured him a glass of milk and set it in front of him.

"You want a beer, too?" she asked Theo.

"No. I want something else."

"Oh, really. And what would that be?"

Jeremy clunked down his empty glass and ran the back of his hand over his milky lips. I'm going to see Dr. Ben.

Do you have to? Ivy signed. It'll be so boring without you, just with old Theo.

Jeremy giggled again and took off.

"Boring?" Theo said. "I beg your pardon."

"Well, do something interesting."

He took a tentative half step toward her. Then he dipped his finger into the giant bowl of fruitcake mix, took two quick steps until he was almost on top of her, and applied the batter to the bridge of her nose.

"Hey!" she said, obviously expecting something else.

"Not interesting enough for you? How about this?" He leaned forward and smooched her on the nose, inhaling most of the batter. "Hey, you weren't kidding. This stuff is good."

She shook her head, laughing. "I would have given you a bite the regular way."

"Ah, but that wouldn't have been interesting, would it?"

Quickly, she dipped her own finger in the bowl and put

some batter on his nose, then stepped closer and slurped it off. As she stood back to get a better look at him, he scooped up more batter but, in aiming for her nose, missed and laid it on her cheek, just at the corner of her mouth.

Slowly, watching her carefully, he leaned forward. She stood completely still, waiting. Deliberately, he missed the batter and pressed his lips on hers. Her eyes closed and she leaned in to him in a boneless, relaxed way, bringing her hands up onto his shoulders. He raised his head, licked the batter off her cheek, and then kissed her again, with the sweet taste between them.

When they came apart, she took a deep breath and said, "Well, finally."

He rested his forehead against hers. "Oh, is that something you've been waiting for?"

"We're not going to play games, are we? You know it is. And you've been waiting, too. If your poor father had stayed healthy, it would have happened long before now. And you know it. Right?"

He sighed. "Right."

"So, how's he doing? Your dad?" She linked her hands behind his neck, letting him know she wasn't letting him get away.

"It's hard to tell. He's not like he used to be, that's for sure, and that's how I want him to be. He's tired, he's clumsy, he drags his foot when he walks. He has trouble signing with his left hand." Theo's voice cracked when he said this. He cleared his throat while Ivy's hands tightened around him. He tried again. "He can't do his magic. I watch him, sitting there with a blanket on his knees and a couple of quarters in his lap. He tries to roll them and hide them and pull them out of the air like he used to. And he can't. He drops them every time."

"Oh, dear," Ivy breathed. "Well, it's early still. He could come a long way back yet. There's time."

"And Palma's acting like a lunatic, all over him one minute and locked in her studio for hours the next. I think she's afraid of him, the way he is now, and I know she's afraid to be alone with him. When I was leaving the house this afternoon, she forbid me to go."

"My goodness. But you did anyway."

"As I said to Jeremy, what's she going to do—kill us?"

"And how's Jeremy?"

"Anxious. Worried. Watchful, always wondering when the other shoe's going to drop. But he's a lot easier to cheer up than Palma. All it takes is cookies and a beer."

She smiled up at him and kissed the corner of his mouth. "And how are you?"

"Anxious. Worried. Exhausted. Resentful. Scared to death." The door to his heart was wide open and it felt good. Ivy could come as far in as she wanted to. He'd never trusted anyone as much as he trusted her at that moment.

She kissed the other corner of his mouth. "Poor Theo. It's so hard."

She couldn't have said anything more right.

"This helps," he said, and pulled her against him. She hung on.

"Your mom's going to have to get a grip pretty soon. Either that, or your dad is going to have to make a full recovery."

"No kidding." But the concerns of his parents were rapidly receding in his mind.

"I mean for when you go off to school."

Reality rushed back.

He pushed her away from him, enough so that he could see her face. "How can I go off to school after this? No matter how much I might want to, it would be cruel. And irresponsible."

She took her hands off his neck. "And what if your dad is really disabled? For keeps? What are you going to do—live at home forever?"

"Come on, Ivy. I don't need this right now. I can't think one *day* ahead, never mind one year."

"Don't be mad, Theo." She put her hands on his forearms, pulling him toward her again. "I'm trying to look out for you—because it sure doesn't seem like anybody else is. The world hasn't stopped because Thomas is sick, even if it feels to you like it has. College application deadlines are still going to come. Aren't you glad you took your SATs before this happened?"

"I don't know. I guess so," he muttered. He let his arms hang at his sides.

"Okay," she said, running her hands up and down his arms. "I won't bug you anymore. At least not today. Why don't you put some more fruitcake batter on me? Anywhere you like. Go for it."

He just stood, his head down, thinking. As far as he could tell, his world *had* stopped. He saw nothing in his future but more of what he'd done since Thomas's stroke—taken care of things and made arrangements and worried. If there was a way out of it, he couldn't see it. College, even if he lived at home while he went, had begun to seem like a dream. And mathematical theories belonged in another, impractical, carefree universe. What did they have to do with anything?

When he didn't answer, she said, "Well, how about if I put some on you?" She took a tiny dip and rubbed it across his lips, then kissed him on top of it.

Sometimes the body has a wisdom that eludes the mind.

14

He lay in bed, fighting sleep as he had since Thomas came home from the hospital, half listening for a cry, a thump, a sound of emergency. Palma, in the same room, in the same *bed* as Thomas, would hear nothing even if he could trust her to be efficient in a crisis.

With the other half of his mind, he thought about Ivy. Of all the times in his life for this to happen, for him to— well, to do whatever he was doing with Ivy—why now, when everything else was so complicated that he barely had time to see her. And whatever he was doing with her was plenty complicated all by itself. He thought about her all the time he wasn't thinking about Thomas. He remembered almost everything she said, and he couldn't get over how great she was with Jeremy—never mind how great she was with the Cooper sisters and Harry and Hazel and the rest of her customers. And he admired her culinary talents and her business acumen and her wit and her dimple—

and at the same time he found himself worrying about how he felt about her. It was too good for him to trust it. Did they really have anything special going on, or was she just a live version of one of his mental vacations—something he needed to take his mind off the heavy dose of reality he was getting? Would she spoil everything by starting in with that MIT stuff again? Was she likely to get sick of him as he became more and more of a plodding drudge?

Still, he grabbed all the time with her he could. At school, they snatched minutes between classes or at lunch, or on the bus, to do what seemed like nothing, but was really the biggest thing there was: pretending that everything was normal.

Once Theo was in the front door of his house, nothing was normal. Palma had tried hiring companions for Thomas so that she could escape to her studio, but communication was such a problem that this hadn't worked very well, and no one had lasted more than two or three days.

One afternoon, Theo came home to Thomas sobbing in frustration because he couldn't lift the tray from the kitchen counter that held his afternoon snack, the one the doctor had insisted he have every day to help him regain his strength. The contents of a plate of grapes, crackers, and almonds lay scattered across the tray, and a broken glass lay on the counter with milk dripping to the floor.

Theo dropped his backpack and helped Thomas to

a chair before cleaning up the mess. Then he brought Thomas his snack and asked, **Where's**—he had to stop and think who the latest companion was—**Russell?**

He left. Palma actually pushed him out the door when she got upset with him. His signing was slow and effortful.

Why was she upset?

Because he didn't understand what she wanted.

So where is she now? Why didn't she help you with the snack?

She went to her studio. She needed to calm down. I told her I could fix my own snack. But I couldn't. And he began to cry again.

Theo had learned that unstable emotions were part of the territory of a stroke victim, but right now that knowledge was meaningless. Seeing his father in tears tore his heart. To him Thomas had always been everything that was big, competent, controlled, content. Now he was as uncertain as a child. And Theo, who only wanted to be a kid, had to be the one who was big and competent. Had that job ever felt as huge and impossible to Thomas as it did to him?

He patted his father's back and handed him a Kleenex. "It's okay, Dad," he said aloud, unable to sign because his hands were busy, knowing his father couldn't hear him, but needing to hear some reassurance, however synthetic, for himself.

As soon as Thomas was settled again, Theo went storming out to Palma's studio in spite of the fact that he and Jeremy had been banned from there all their lives, to enter only by Palma's rare invitation. But today was different. He couldn't wait for her to emerge at her own leisurely whim. Of course, she couldn't hear him if he knocked on the door, so he had no choice but to simply let himself in.

She sat with her back to him, her head in her hands, low, guttural sounds coming from her. He realized she was crying.

Great. A day that set a record. Both parents crying within the same hour.

He looked around the studio and saw, along with the customary creative "orderly disorder," as Palma called it, of sculptures in different stages of completion, mangled lumps of clay heaped at her work stations, piles that looked as if they had been mashed and beaten with blunt instruments.

He put his hand on her shoulder, and she jumped.

I'm sorry. I didn't mean to startle you.

Quickly she swiped at the tears on her cheeks and stood to face him.

What happened with Russell? Theo asked.

On her feet, Palma seemed her formidable self again, hopped up with fire and indignation. **Oh, Russell. He was useless. Couldn't understand anything I wanted.**

Did you write him a note?

Palma was self-conscious about her writing. Because the grammar and syntax of sign language were so much different from those of English, she hated the inevitable mistakes she made, thinking they made her appear ignorant. And naturally, the less she wrote, the more likely she was to make mistakes when she did.

Why should I? I was paying him to understand what we wanted. He was the one who was supposed to try.

But you ended up leaving Thomas all alone. He can't do that yet. No one wanted to suggest that maybe Thomas never would be able to do that.

But I have to do my work. If there had been a way to indicate a wail in sign language, that sentence could have contained it. **I can't do everything.**

As far as Theo could see, Palma not only wasn't doing everything—she was hardly doing anything.

You've got to come out now and talk to Pop. He's very upset.

I can't. She sat down, her arms folded across her chest.

What do you mean? He needs you.

She unfolded her arms. **And I need him.** The wail was there again somehow. **He's always taken care of me. He knows what I have to have to do my work.**

Well, get over it, Theo thought.

Palma. Mother. Don't you get it? Everything's different now. Pop's not the only one who has to make adjustments. You have to step up now.

I can't. I won't. She wasn't just acting like a spoiled child, Theo realized. She *was* one. Spoiled first by her indulgent parents, and then by everybody else who fell under her spell, dazzled by her beauty and her talent and her mercurial charm. How did you get someone to grow up when she didn't want to?

You have to. I can't manage everything. You're the grownup, not me.

She looked up at him, pleading in her eyes.

No, I'm not. I'm not anything without Thomas.

How dare she be as frightened and distraught and disappointed as he was? How dare she lie down and refuse to cope? It was such a spineless, weak-willed abdication he wanted to kick her. Why did she get to bail out of the unholy mess when he couldn't?

You can take care of things, she signed. **You're better at it than I am. You're better. You can hear.**

Theo almost gasped. Palma's position had always been that deafness elevated people, made them more sensitive and attentive, more observant, more appreciative. He knew there were those in the Deaf Club who thought hearies were superior in many, mysterious ways, but Palma always seemed to regard him, Theo, as the one with the handicap, though the perfect one for relieving her of chores she didn't want to be bothered with.

He remembered Thomas's telling him, "You're not hearing, you're not deaf. You're just you," and knowing that being "just you" was fine and dandy. With Palma he was never sure—he was lacking because he could hear, but as a hearie he had abilities that she valued. So "just you" was never just right. Now she was telling him he was better? Had she thought that all along?

While he gaped, she lowered her head and wouldn't look at him. When he knelt in front of her and put his hands before her face to force her to look at his signing, she squeezed her eyes tightly shut.

He got the message loud and clear in the silence. He rose and left the studio, crossing back through the yard to the house, where he would take care of his father. And of everything else.

The next day at school, in the few minutes before their first class, Theo told Ivy about the latest developments.

"I could just throttle your mother," Ivy said. "If you'll excuse me for saying so. What's wrong with her? Nobody likes this situation, that goes without saying, but she's letting all of you down. I do your cooking and you do everything else while she does nothing."

"Jeremy's been doing the laundry," Theo put in.

"Oh, terrific. I'll bet that's had its humorous moments. The red sock in with the white underwear—has that happened yet?"

"Not that specific adventure. But we've had a few things go into the dryer that shouldn't have, and they ended up looking like doll clothes."

"Surely your mother could do laundry. It's not that hard."

"I don't think Jeremy would agree."

The first bell rang, and Ivy stood on her tiptoes to give him a quick kiss before dashing off. Public displays of affection had always embarrassed him when he'd been a witness to them. Now that he was a participant, he thought they should occur more often.

Even Ivy's loyalty couldn't quiet his buzzing mind, or answer the question of how he was to manage. Taking care of everything was hard enough now while he was a student and had some flexibility. What would happen when he finished school and had to get a job and be gone even more than he was now? What would happen if Thomas had another stroke? How was he to handle Palma when his resentment toward her increased logarithmically every day?

After school, he was sitting slumped at the bus stop waiting for Ivy when she came skipping up to him.

"What?" he asked. "You got an A on your history test?"

"Yes, but that's not what's up with me." She kissed him

and bounced on her toes in front of him. "Ask me who's the most brilliant person you know."

"Who? But I have an idea I know the answer."

"Who do you think?"

"Could it possibly be—you?"

She kissed him again. "Followed closely by you."

The bus pulled up with squealing brakes and gusts of diesel breath, and then the shoving contest that was boarding began. They weren't able to talk again until they were settled in their seats. Ivy turned to him and took both his hands in hers.

"I have the answer to your problem."

"Which of my vast assortment of problems might you be referring to?"

"About somebody to take care of your dad."

"Well, don't keep it to yourself. Tell."

"Harry and Hazel. They can sign enough to make better than basic communications, and they'd learn even faster if they were signing more often and with others than just me. They've got plenty of time on their hands, and they'd love to feel useful."

"What makes you think they would have the slightest interest in spending their days with a crazy woman and a sad old guy?"

"Who do you think would have more compassion than them? They've lived long enough to have seen plenty of sad and hard things. They know it's just luck that keeps them from being like your father. And you know them—they have tons of energy and enthusiasm. They'd be perfect."

"You're still missing a big part of this equation—like would they want to."

"Equation," she said, putting her hands on her heart and fluttering her eyelashes. "I love it when you talk mathematics to me." Then she straightened up. "Well, is it okay if I ask them?"

"Sure, I guess so. Though I can't even guess how Palma would feel about it. She's been pretty hard on the companions from the agency."

"What does she care who's there, as long as they can sign so she doesn't have to write notes, and as long as they take up the slack that she's letting pile up. Is that a mixed metaphor?"

"I don't know. But it could add up. If Palma goes for it, and if Harry and Hazel do, too."

"Add up," she said, sighing. "More mathematics talk."

15

When Theo came in the door from school, Jeremy was there in the living room with Thomas, watching TV.

Where's Palma? Theo asked, furious, as soon as he'd put his books down.

What's wrong? Jeremy signed.

She kept you out of school, didn't she?

I don't mind, Jeremy signed timidly.

I know. That's part of the problem.

For the second time in two days he did the forbidden—he walked into Palma's studio without an invitation. This time she was at her worktable with a pile of clay in front of her. She was looking into the mirror on the wall next to her, the one she used to observe her hands while she worked on the sculpture of whatever sign she'd chosen. This time as she looked in the mirror, she was making, over and over, the very expressive sign for *scared*, her two spread hands placed over her heart. As soon as she saw Theo, she let her hands drop, then raised them again. **What?**

He thought she looked scared. And unkempt, which wasn't like her. A diva's appearance always mattered—she never even came down for her coffee in the mornings without lipstick and mascara, and her hair done. Now her hair actually looked dirty. And her face, without makeup, looked tired and old. If he'd seen her on the street, he wasn't sure he'd have recognized her.

Don't you remember you're not to come in here without an invitation? She signed the question with some of her old fire.

He wasn't even going to get involved with that when there was such a bigger problem at hand. **You said you wouldn't keep Jeremy out of school anymore. He needs to go. It's not his job to take care of Dad.**

She threw her hands up, not in any formal sign, but in the universal one of helplessness.

Theo's hands moved fast, the way they always did when he was angry or excited. **What if I told you I might have found somebody who can help? Somebody who can sign a little?**

Who? Her signing was tight and suspicious.

More than one person. A brother and sister, both retired, that Ivy's been teaching to sign. They might be able to help.

They can hear?

Yes.

But they can sign, too?

A little. Enough. They're interested in learning more and getting better. You could help them. He wasn't so angry that he didn't recognize that a bribe to her vanity might help his argument.

She considered. **Can they come tomorrow?**

I don't know. I'll see. He turned and left the studio before she could remember she was sore about his coming in without an invitation. He sure hoped she'd checked out credentials for baby-sitters for him and Jeremy when they were small a little better than she just had for Harry and Hazel. All she'd seemed to care about was that they were available. But then he remembered, Thomas had been the one to arrange for the sitters. And Thomas was always very careful with what he loved.

Ivy came by with dinner later in the afternoon.

"Did you talk to Harry and Hazel? What did they say?" he asked as she unpacked her insulated bag.

"They're not sure. It makes them nervous. They have friends who've had strokes, and they don't think they can do heavy lifting and nursing and stuff like that."

"They don't have to. The physical therapist and the visiting nurse do the medical stuff. And he's completely mobile, just slow. All they'd have to do is keep him company, help with snacks, make sure he takes his medicine on time, get him out for a walk. Baby-sitting stuff, just until he gets his strength back. If they could start tomorrow, that'd be great."

"Well, let me call them." She picked up the phone and talked while Theo put various things either in the oven or in the refrigerator, and set the table.

She hung up. "Okay. They said they'd try it. No promises yet, but I told them how desperate you are. I hope you don't mind, but I made Palma sound like a real dragon. Don't look like that—it's part of my strategy. You know how Harry loves a challenge. I just thought it'd be more interesting for him if I gave him a dragon to slay."

"It's not much of an exaggeration lately. I used to complain about her being a prima donna, but I prefer that to this poor-me-I-just-can't-handle-it thing she's got going on now."

"I was just trying to lay the groundwork so they wouldn't be surprised if she turns out to be really hard to deal with. I also turned your dad into a saint. I hope that's okay."

"It's not only okay, it's true."

"I'll go in and say hi to him before I leave. Anyway, I need to give Jeremy some snoogies. I know he misses me."

"I miss you, too. Can I have some snoogies, whatever they are?"

"You doing anything tomorrow night?" She gave him a farcical leer, flashing her dimple. "I could come over after dinner and show you."

"We'll see how things go with Harry, Hazel, and company. I may be cleaning up after a massacre."

"I do love an optimistic person," she said, heading for the living room.

Theo made sure Jeremy got off to school the next morning, but hung around himself until Harry and Hazel arrived at ten. He introduced them to Palma, who signed in such a slow, exaggerated way that even he could hardly understand her. It reminded him of the way hearies exaggerated their lip movements when speaking to deaf people—something they all hated—thinking it made lip reading easier, when all it did was make it impossible, and looked funny besides. Thomas's current signing might have been halting, but it was still more natural than Palma's was that morning.

From the way Harry and Hazel watched Palma, Ivy must have really done a number on her. They looked as if they expected her to burst into flames at any moment. When she took off for her studio, they visibly relaxed.

They listened with all four ears to everything Theo said and wrote down everything he told them about medicines, food, exercise, and safety precautions. When he finished, Harry handed Theo his cell phone.

"What's this for?"

"Take it and go on to school. We'll be fine. And if we're not, we'll call you. Now get out of here."

Theo stood, hesitant, watching the three of them.

Hazel signed to Thomas something she'd clearly rehearsed carefully: **Do you play checkers?**

Thomas nodded.

Hazel pumped her fist and said, "Yes!" Then she signed, **Want to play for money?**

Thomas pumped his good fist and signed, **Yes**, a movement of the fist up and down, like a nodding head.

"Hey, Harry," Hazel said. "Break out the board. And your wallet."

Theo left for school, the cell phone in his pocket and hope in his heart.

He rushed home after school, having spent the whole day with his hand in his pocket, clutching the phone, waiting for it to ring. Jeremy was already there, sitting at the kitchen table with Hazel, one of his old picture books laid open between them. Jeremy patiently "read" the story to Hazel, stopping to watch her imitate his signs, then correcting her when necessary.

"Hi, Theo," she said, looking up when he came in. **Want a drink?** "Didn't I get that right?" she asked when Jeremy collapsed, giggling, on the table.

"Actually, you asked me if I wanted either a beer, or a drunk. I don't care for either just now, but thanks for the offer." He demonstrated the sign for *drink*.

Hazel bopped Jeremy on the top of the head with the picture book.

"What's Ivy been teaching you, anyway?" Theo asked.

"Our last lesson was on food and drink. I got a little mixed up, that's all."

Jeremy raised his head, made the sign for *drunk*, and started laughing all over again.

"Tell him I'm happy I can be so entertaining," Hazel said, and then watched closely as Theo signed, imitating his signs with her own hands.

"How did it go today?" Theo asked. "Where are Harry and Pop?"

"Those guys have a checkers marathon going on. Harry'll be lucky if he gets out of here with the shirt on his back."

"No kidding. It's been a long time since I've played checkers with Pop. I didn't know he was that good."

"Maybe it's Harry who's so bad. But who cares? They've been having a good time. Every time Thomas signs something Harry doesn't understand, Thomas has to write it out for him, so maybe it's good therapy for your dad. And Harry's learned a lot of new words, most of which I wouldn't want him using in polite company."

"So no problems?"

"The only problem I had was getting them to stop long enough for lunch and a walk."

"Did Palma come out for lunch?"

"Not with us. She must have had something while we were out walking because there were extra dishes in the sink when we got back."

Involuntarily, Theo glanced at the spotless sink. "You didn't have to clean up. I can do that when I get home. You just have to see to Pop."

Hazel flapped her hand. "Don't be silly. What am I supposed to do while they're playing checkers like fiends? Besides, this place needs a little . . . fluffing," she said tactfully.

"Yeah, well, Pop's always done most of that. Palma's funny about having other people around unless they can sign, so we've never had somebody to help with the house who stayed very long." He paused. "Palma can be a bit temperamental."

"So Ivy said."

"Well, thanks. About the dishes. And everything."

"Don't give it a second thought. Now, do you want us to clear out, or to hang around so you can do your homework or whatever?"

"You must have things you need to do at home."

"What? Ivy's bringing dinner. I get up at six and all my housework's done by seven-thirty. We can stay awhile if you need us to."

"Does this mean you'll be coming back tomorrow?" Theo asked hesitantly. He was afraid to hope.

"I don't know why not," Hazel said. "I don't want to be

the one responsible for busting up this checkers-a-thon."

He wanted to throw himself to his knees and kiss her hands. "And after that?" he asked with trepidation. "I don't know how long we'll need you, but I'm hoping he'll be able to manage on his own before too long."

"As much as you want us, I guess."

"You mean you'd be willing to come every day?"

"If that's what you want. Harry and I can trade off if one of us has something else to do during the day."

"I think it would be easiest that way. For Pop. So he doesn't have to keep getting used to somebody new. If that's okay with you."

"Now, don't be a bonehead, Theo. I told you it was. And you know I wouldn't bamboozle you."

"Bamboozle?"

"I bet you don't have a sign for that."

"I bet you're right. Well, great. That's great. Wow. Thanks."

What's happening? Jeremy signed.

Harry and Hazel are going to come every day to help with Pop.

You mean they'll be here when I get home from school?

Yes. Is that okay with you?

Yeah. I like them. But is it still okay if I go over to Dr. Ben's sometimes to work on the airplanes?

Sure. I like to go over there, too. Maybe we could

bring Pop. It might cheer him up. He can still fly them even if he can't build them so easily anymore.

Maybe Harry and Hazel could come too.

We'll see. We don't want to inconvenience Dr. Ben by bringing a whole circus over there.

Well, I know you don't go over there to see the airplanes.

You got that right, Einstein. He took hold of Jeremy's cowlick and gave it a yank.

Theo wandered into the dining room, where Thomas and Harry sat across from each other, concentrating hard. Thomas raised his head and grinned at Theo. The right half of his mouth went all the way up and the left half went only partway up, which gave him a somewhat diabolical look. But it was the first real smile Theo had seen on his face in the month since his stroke.

Who's winning? he asked.

Don't ask, Harry signed.

Not you, I take it.

Harry turned a little pad toward Theo. There were two columns, one labeled HARRY and the other THOMAS. There were a few numbers on Harry's side, but many more on Thomas's.

"He told me he hadn't played in years," Harry said.

Theo signed this for Thomas, who grinned again and signed, True, his index finger coming away from his lips. Guess I'm just smart.

Harry signed, **Tomorrow I'll be smart, too.**

Tomorrow? Thomas asked. **You'll be back?**

You chicken? Harry asked.

Not me. Are you?

Not me.

Okay, Thomas signed. **Good.**

As Theo went to the door with Harry and Hazel, he was almost stammering with gratitude. "I can't thank—you know he hasn't smiled since—Harry, you don't have to let him win all the time."

Harry looked offended. "I wish I *was* letting him win. He beat me fair and square, darn it."

"Yeah, right. Well, I don't have to know. It's between you two. Hey, we need to talk about money, too. Not checkers money, but the real stuff, employment salaries. I don't know what Ivy said to you about that, but I—"

"Ivy didn't say anything," Harry said. "As for us, we don't need the cash. This is something we want to do."

"Sorry," Theo said. "I can't let you do it for nothing. I wouldn't feel right. I know it's not easy, taking care of a sick person. You know we're hoping it'll be temporary, but we don't know how long a temporary."

Hazel put her hand on Theo's arm. "We hope it's temporary, too. And we know you know how hard the job is—though I have to say today didn't seem all that hard. So why don't you just pay us whatever you think is fair, if you really think you have to pay us anything at all."

"Okay. I can do that. Maybe then Harry'll be able to cover his gambling debts."

"I'm getting even tomorrow. You tell Thomas that. What time you want us?"

After they left, Theo went back to the kitchen, where Thomas and Jeremy were eating apples and crackers at the table.

Want a drunk? Jeremy asked, and cracked himself up all over again.

16

After less than two weeks of the new arrangement, Theo felt as if he had come out of a long, dark tunnel with Harry and Hazel as the sunshine at the end of it. Jeremy loved them, and Thomas loved them even more, since Harry kept losing money to him. Theo had gotten his own cell phone in case of emergencies, but he no longer felt so sure that one was always just about to happen.

Theo had stayed home every afternoon after they left just to make sure everything was going smoothly, and had seen Ivy only at school, and briefly, when she brought dinner over. It wasn't enough.

Palma had made herself scarce for the whole time. She was usually around when Harry and Hazel showed up in the morning, primarily because Theo forbade her to go to her studio until then, leaving Thomas alone. But once they were there, she disappeared and stayed gone all day, sneaking out of the studio for lunch while the others took their walk.

"Doesn't that seem odd to you?" Ivy asked at school on Friday. "Sort of paranoid or something?"

"Well, that's Palma for you," Theo said. "I've got to say, things have been a lot calmer around our place with her stashed away. I hope she's creating like crazy, making lots of expensive masterpieces, and not just sulking in there with a chip on her shoulder."

"I just don't get her. She should be thrilled. Harry and Hazel are the answer to a prayer. And your dad seems happy with them."

"He's ecstatic. Winning all that money from Harry makes him feel competent again, and so does being able to help them learn more sign. He even seems to be getting stronger now that they're making sure he gets some exercise every day. And Jeremy's latched on to Hazel like a long-lost relative."

"What about you, cupcake?" she asked. "Feeling better?"

"Well, I'm sleeping all night again. Haven't had a disaster dream in a while. Maybe I've turned a corner. If I have, you're to thank for it."

"I'll remind you of that every few minutes so you don't forget how valuable I am."

"No chance of that." He watched her scrape the last of her yogurt out of the carton with a plastic spoon. He remembered how hard he'd tried to stay out of her way at first, when he'd thought she was deaf. What an idiot he'd been. And probably still was. But Ivy didn't seem to care. In spite of everything else going on, in one big way he felt lucky. He had Ivy.

"Let's do something Saturday night," he said. "I've served enough time under house arrest. Palma can do the duty for a change."

"She has to get used to it sooner or later. You need a life. Saturday night for sure."

Saturday night was definitely not all right with Palma.

He'd been foolishly, blindly hopeful that he could treat this Saturday night like any other; that he could just tell her he was going out and then go, the way he'd been able to do before Thomas's train wreck.

I have to work. You've got to stay home. Her eyes were big and glittering and intense.

I've been home forever. I'm going out. It wouldn't kill her to take a night off from work, he thought. And it might kill me if I don't.

She grabbed his arm, then released it to sign, **Then get those people, whatever their names are, to come. I can't be alone here.**

It's Saturday. I can't ask them. And their names, as you very well know, are Harry and Hazel.

Ask them. You have to. Tears spilled from her eyes and tracked mascara tragically down her cheeks.

"Oh, for God's sake," Theo said, and reached for the phone.

Harry answered, even though Theo had dialed Hazel's number.

"Oh, hi, Theo. What's up?"

Theo explained.

"Well, we're having a little card party here—"

"Never mind, then," Theo said hastily. "We'll figure out something."

"Now, hold on," Harry said. "I didn't say we couldn't help. We've got Adele and Rochelle here, and Molly and Paul, our across-the-street neighbors. We could bring them along. Just move our party to your house, if that's okay with you. We'd be glad to have Thomas and Jeremy join us. Your mother, too, if she wanted to."

Theo didn't even bother to consult with Palma, to find out if having the whole party come was okay with her. He was going out with Ivy, that's all there was to it. And he'd agree to having the entire membership of the Hell's Angels come over if it got him out the door.

"Sure. That sounds fine. When can you get here?"

"Half hour or less. We've got to pack up our snacks and drinks and stuff. Hang on, Theo. Reinforcements are on the way."

They were there in twenty-five minutes, six old friends with young attitudes, a traveling carnival of good spirits and frisky minds.

They had their card party set up so fast Theo wondered if Harry had ever been a dealer in Las Vegas. While he made introductions, Hazel laid out places for Thomas and Jeremy, Adele poured drinks, Rochelle arranged snacks, and Molly and Paul learned how to sign *hello* to Theo and Jeremy. Harry fastened a green eyeshade around his head.

Where'd you get that thing? Thomas asked. **Aren't you caught in a time warp?**

If you find a time you like, Harry signed, **I say stick with it.**

"You think you're going to be okay?" Theo asked.

"Get out of here," Harry said, dealing cards. "We need to concentrate."

Adele and Rochelle absently waved at him as they studied the cards in their hands. As far as the others were concerned, he'd already left.

Ivy was waiting for him at her house with her coat on. "Let's get going. Seconds count when you're on the lam."

"No argument." He grabbed her hand and they ran to the car. He felt as if he really was on the lam, in some black-and-white forties gangster movie. "We're going to go eat and then go to the movies, and then take a walk by the river, and stick up a liquor store if you want, or maybe you'd prefer a gourmet shop, and then—"

"I can take it from there, pineapple," she said, squeezing his hand. "And we're not going to talk about anybody's illness or problems or arrangements. Tonight nobody else is on the map."

He started the car. "Pineapple?"

"It's a term of endearment used by Charles II for one of his mistresses. In the 1600s pineapples were a lot more rare and special than they are now."

"So does that mean the person you use it on now is rare and special, or that he's not?"

"This isn't rocket science, pineapple. Maybe you could figure it out better if it was."

"I'll take it as a compliment, then."

She leaned her head against his shoulder. "That's my genius."

It was late when Theo got home, but the lights were still on in the living room. When Theo came in, he saw Jeremy asleep on the couch and Thomas, with Harry's green eyeshade on, sitting behind a pile of poker chips.

Thank goodness, Harry signed when he saw Theo. **We've got to get out of here while we still have gas money.**

Hazel pushed her chair back and yawned. **Time for us to go home, Thomas. We'll see you on Monday.**

As the others gathered up their cards and party gear, Theo said to Harry, "Thanks a million. I'll add these hours to the weekly ones."

"Don't you dare," Harry said. "This was for fun. I don't think of your father as just a sick guy who needs care. I think of him as a pal. And you should, too. How'd you like to be nothing but somebody's problem?"

That question didn't really seem to require an answer, so Theo asked instead, "Did Palma come in?"

"Never saw her. Either she's still working, or there's a back way for her to sneak up to bed. I wish she'd let us show her we're nobody she has to worry about. It's funny—at first, I thought we should worry about her, but now she seems to be worrying about us."

"She's just jumpy around people she can't communicate with. She's not a good lip-reader, so she has to depend on sign."

"Well, what's the big deal? We can sign good enough for Thomas."

"I'll talk to her," Theo said, wondering if there was really any point to it. At that moment, though, he didn't care. The wonder drug of Ivy's company was still working in him, and he hadn't yet resumed his role as the guy who had to keep the whole show on the road.

After they left, he checked the studio and found it empty. He made sure Palma was asleep in her bed before he got Jeremy to his feet and sleep-walked him up to bed. Then he came back for Thomas and helped him up the stairs, too. He could probably have made it by himself, but Theo lived in fear that he'd suffer another stroke while he was on the stairs, or miss a step with his weak leg and fall.

I can get myself to bed, Thomas signed.

You sure? Theo asked. Until now, Theo had helped him undress and put on his pajamas, brush his teeth and get into bed. They were both made uncomfortable by this intimacy, but Thomas needed assistance and Palma refused to do it. She seemed blind to how stricken Theo was by Thomas's helplessness, and how embarrassed Thomas was at needing Theo's help. But tonight, with Palma already asleep, Theo was willing to let Thomas try the bedtime routine himself rather than disturb her with the two of them rambling around the bedroom. Of course, the noise wouldn't bother her, but the lights would, and he was more than willing to let Thomas take the heat for that.

The next morning, Palma was the goddess of righteous wrath.

Who were all those people in my house last night? There are cracker crumbs and peanuts all over the floor. And was someone smoking? It smells funny in here. I can't believe you let your father stay up so late—don't you know he needs his sleep? And then made him get ready for bed all by himself. What were you thinking?

Theo tuned to another mental station while she went on, or else he would have felt like handcuffing her so she couldn't sign at all. He knew no one had smoked, and that the mess, as she was calling it, wasn't anywhere near as bad as what he and Jeremy alone could create in an evening of TV watching. And if she knew Thomas was getting ready for bed by himself, why hadn't she pitched in to help him?

When she finally ran down, he asked, **So what do you want me to do about it? You're the one who insisted on a sitter for Pop.**

Don't call it a sitter, she signed indignantly. **He needs care, not sitting.**

Palma—he took money from those guys last night playing poker. They're the ones who needed care, by the time he got through with them. And staying up a little later than usual was fun for him.

He needs his rest. He must be cared for. She was using such big gestures she might as well have been shouting.

Finally he'd had enough. **He *is* being cared for. And you're not doing any of it. But you're very free with your criticism of those who are. What is your problem?**

To his amazement, Palma burst into tears. He'd always considered that phrase just a figure of speech, but she actually seemed to burst, like a pierced water balloon, with tears almost springing from her eyes. He was so startled he even took a step backward. A moan issued from her and she covered her face with her hands and staggered over to lean against the wall.

Theo couldn't offer her any comfort in words, and he was afraid to try to touch her. All he could do was gape and wait.

After a long time, Palma straightened up and took her hands down from her face. She swiped at her wet cheeks, but wouldn't look at Theo.

Somehow this outburst seemed more authentic than her usual dramatics. He knelt on the floor at her feet and signed up into her bowed face. **What's going on?**

She shook her head.

He remembered the day he'd caught her signing *scared* over and over in the studio mirror. Maybe she hadn't been researching a new sculpture after all. **Are you afraid?** When she didn't answer, he went on, **We all are. But he's getting better.**

Again she shook her head.

Yes. He is. He played poker last night. He got himself ready for bed. His signing is getting better.

But he'll never be the same. She signed in small, tight movements.

That's probably true. Theo didn't want to believe it either, but the facts were there, insisting every day that he do so. **And neither will we. Maybe we'll always be more worried than we used to be. Maybe we'll value each ordinary day more. Maybe we'll—well, I don't know what we'll do. But we're already different. Like they say—you can't unring the bell. But we'll still be okay.** Won't we? he wondered to himself.

I won't. He believed in me. He always told me I was really talented. He was even—she paused, search-

170

ing for the right word—**awed by me. He hasn't told me any of that since he got sick.**

He's had a lot of other things to think about. And you've made yourself pretty scarce. Besides, everybody thinks you're really talented. Theo was puzzled. How could his father's stroke make his mother doubt her talent?

No they don't. They think I'm a novelty. A deaf sculptor who sculpts hands signing. It's quaint. It's quirky. It's interesting. But it's not really art.

What was she talking about? She had a major sold-out show once a year. She'd not only been in all the art magazines, but also in *Time* and *People*, and *The Wall Street Journal*. People overbid each other for her work. How could her work not really be art?

I don't understand, was all he could say.

The only one I really believe is Thomas.

She believed Thomas over all those art experts? Thomas, who, wonderful as he was, was only a furniture maker?

When Theo didn't answer, she signed, **Because he's like me.**

And then he did understand. Thomas was deaf, too. She didn't have to be suspicious of him, or feel inferior or stupid, the way she did with most hearing people.

It was as if a door into her mind had opened for Theo. His parents' relationship, which had always been such a mystery to him, was rooted in Thomas's strength and calmness in the face of Palma's vast insecurities and fears—

the ones he had never seen because she was so busy covering them up with her extravagant behavior. All the carrying-on that had driven him nuts was a way for her to protect herself, a shield to hide behind. And the power of her sculpture of connection, the one that he loved so much, was no accident. It had come from her heart, because of Thomas.

After a quick surge of compassion for his poor frightened mother who couldn't fully believe in and take joy from her own amazing talent—which even he, an artistic dodo, could recognize—he was swamped with fury. How dare she have held them all hostage for so long to her insecurities? Why couldn't she have acted like a grownup instead of forcing that role on him while he was still a little kid? Why couldn't she have just let him *be* a little kid? She could have faked maturity at least as well as he had.

Inside his fury was the tangle of deafness and hearing. What would Palma have been like if she could hear? Still insecure? Was that just a part of who she was, having nothing to do with whether or not she could hear? How could he ever know how much of what she was depended on what she could or couldn't hear, and how much was simply in her genes? It had always been so easy to blame all his family problems on deafness, but how lazy that was, how foolish.

But what did you do with someone who'd made it clear that she wasn't going to embrace the responsibilities of being a grownup, and a parent? She'd leaned on Thomas for most of that, and now that he could no longer fill the role, she was trying to push it off onto Theo. And he couldn't be sure she wouldn't succeed.

She continued to watch him as he stood there, processing all this. She seemed to be waiting for him to tell her something, but he didn't know what it might be. He knew he wasn't going to try to reassure her about her talent. If years of art experts telling her how wonderful she was hadn't done it, his little contribution wasn't going to.

And he was afraid to open his mouth—or his hands— afraid that his fury and frustration with her would spill out before he had a chance to think about the best way to respond.

Slowly, she raised her hands and signed, **I don't want those people coming anymore. Nobody can take care of your father better than you can.**

His mouth dropped open. **That's impossible! I have to go to school. As long as you won't stay here alone with Pop, someone else has to.**

You can get tutored at home. You have to tell the school I need you here.

No. He signed the word so hard, his fingers snapped. **No. No. No. I'll do everything that needs doing after school, but I'm not quitting school.**

You wouldn't be quitting. You'd just be doing it at home.

No. His fingers snapped again. He'd given up enough already and there would be more sacrifice ahead: of college, of the chance to get away from home, to feel free. He wasn't going to let her bully or maneuver him into giving up this one thing he had left for the short time that he still had it.

The tears started down her face again, but this time he was unmoved. This time he saw them as manipulative rather than sincere. He turned his back on her and went upstairs to his room two steps at a time. He stood, looking at the pile of college catalogs and half-completed applications on his desk. With one sweep of his arm, he shoved them all off his desk and into the trash can. Then he grabbed his jacket and pounded back down the stairs.

As he steamed past the living room, Palma rushed out and tried to grab him by the arm. He shook her off and kept going, slamming the front door after him. Even if she couldn't hear that, he thought, she ought to be able to feel it. He hoped it shook the whole house.

17

He got to Ivy's on his bike in record-breaking time. He leaned on the doorbell, drumming his fingers on the door-frame, then leaned on the bell again, long after it was clear that no one was home.

He slammed his open hand on the doorframe and turned back down the steps. Where *was* she? He'd gotten so used to finding her at work in the kitchen that he was out-raged to discover she wasn't there now, when he needed so much to talk to her.

The library? Flying planes with her father? Taking a walk? He didn't know where to start.

While he stood on the sidewalk wondering where to go next, a car, with Ivy at the wheel, pulled up to the curb. Dr. Roper got out on the passenger side.

Hi, Theo. Good timing. You want to come in? It's cold out here.

Hi. Yes, I'd like to come in. Thanks.

Ivy locked the car and came around to the sidewalk. "Hi." Then she took a closer look at him. "Are you okay? What's going on?"

"I need to talk to you. Where have you been?"

"It's Sunday, remember? We were at church and then out to breakfast. Just like we are every Sunday morning." She gave him another close look. "You better get in there and tell me what's happening."

They went in and hung up their coats, and Ivy and Theo went into the kitchen while Dr. Roper went upstairs.

"Want something hot?" Ivy asked.

"How about some hot buttered hemlock?"

"Hey," she said. "Things can't be that bad." She poured milk into a saucepan and got out the cocoa. "Okay. Talk."

"Can you think of anyone who might suggest that I drop out of school to take care of my dad?"

Ivy turned to him. "No! She didn't."

He nodded.

"But what about Harry and Hazel? I thought that was working out."

"It was. It is. But Palma's not happy having strangers around—even if they can sign. I'm not sure she knows what good signers they are. She barely comes out of her hole when they're there."

"Theo." Her voice was severe. "You can't let her get away with this. If you give in now, you're done for. You'll never get away."

"Are you nuts? How can I even think about getting away? Who's going to keep things going at home?"

"How about Palma? Why does she get off the hook and you have to have it right through your neck?"

"What happens to Pop and Jeremy if I *do* leave and Palma *doesn't* pick up the slack?"

"Why don't you find out?"

"Be serious. I can't do that. What if Pop falls down the stairs ten minutes after I pack up and leave?"

"What makes you think he's not falling down the stairs right now? The fact that you're in the neighborhood doesn't mean you can protect everybody from everything. You're not Superman."

"I'm the closest thing to it he's got. I'm the closest they've all got."

She brought him a cup of cocoa and sat down next to him. "I hate to break this to you, but there are other people who can do what you're doing. And maybe do it better."

He was quiet, looking into his cup. Then he said, "What if it was your dad? There's just the two of you. Could you leave him with somebody else? Some stranger?"

"That's not a fair question," she said quietly.

"*Fair* is a word that's not in my vocabulary anymore. It doesn't exist in the real world. Stuff you think isn't fair still happens to you and there's nothing you can do about it."

Ivy stood up, paced around the kitchen, sat down, and

stood up again. "But this *is* something you have some control over."

"Hey," Theo said, setting his mug down so hard the cocoa spilled on the tabletop. "I came over here thinking I'd get some understanding."

"I'm trying to help you. We're talking about the rest of your life. What are you waiting for? When are you going to start taking care of yourself? Or are you getting some big fat sense of being necessary and essential and indispensable out of all this? Maybe you're the one with the problem. Maybe you need all this and you don't really want to find out that they can get along without you. You know, in the Orkney Islands the geese being driven to market were walked through pitch and then through sand to make their own boots for the long walk. What if they'd refused? What if they hadn't let themselves be victimized? Maybe they wouldn't have ended up with their necks wrung."

"You think those geese had a choice? You think they even knew what was happening? Maybe what they were doing was preparing themselves for the unavoidable as well as they could." Was he really arguing with her about geese?

He stood now, too. "If we're going to get personal, what about you?"

"Me? What do you mean?"

"All this cooking and serving you do. Don't you know what that's all about? What it's got to do with your mother?"

"I don't know what you're talking about." But before she turned away from him, he saw an expression of sharp pain cross her face.

"Nurturing, that's what I'm talking about. Love. Food as love. Weren't you paying attention in English when we talked about metaphors?"

She said nothing, just kept her back turned to him.

"Haven't you figured out yet that no matter how many people you feed, no matter how maternal you are with your cooking, you can't be the substitute for a mother who should be doing the same for you?"

"I think you'd better go home now," she said in an icy voice.

"I think so, too." He found his jacket and left, closing the front door quietly behind him.

He got on his bike and began riding aimlessly. A cold wind blew into his face, but he already felt so cold from the inside out he hardly noticed it.

What did Ivy mean, he had control over what was happening? What control? Palma was perfectly capable of throwing Harry and Hazel out the next time they came to help. It was her house, after all, and she had the right. And, no matter what he thought, he was still a minor and she was still his mother. She got to make the rules.

And then there were Thomas and Jeremy. Leaving them uncared for was something he knew he couldn't do. Like the Cooper sisters said, family first, work second.

As for Ivy—well, he should have listened to his instincts the first time he saw her. He knew he shouldn't have gotten involved with her, but his stupid hormones weren't listening to him. Funny that it wasn't the deafness thing that turned out to be the problem, the way he thought it would be, but something much more universal—a failure to understand each other even though they could both hear and had two languages in common. Or maybe that wasn't what it was. To tell the truth, he wasn't really sure what had happened between them. Just that it was bad and seemed too big to fix. And what was that stuff about geese?

Finally, there was nothing to do but go home. No matter how much he didn't want to, what else was he going to do? He had four dollars in his pocket and seventeen years of responsible habits on his shoulders. And what if Thomas *had* fallen down the stairs while he was gone and Palma was hiding out someplace?

When he came in, Jeremy was in the front hall, buttoning Thomas into his overcoat.

We're taking a walk. We're going over to Dr. Ben's to look at the airplanes. Maybe we can fly some.

Whose idea was this? Theo asked.

Jeremy handed Thomas his scarf and watched while he wound it, one-handed, around his neck. **Dr. Ben called and asked if we wanted to come over. He said he'd missed us but didn't want to disturb us while Pop was**

getting better. I told him Pop was ready to fly. Want to come?

No, thanks. Have fun.

After they left, Theo went upstairs, plowed through the mess on the floor, and flung himself on his lumpy, unmade bed. What was he doing, letting a kid take a sick man out in the cold for a long walk? Why was he bothering to come home if he wasn't going to take the responsibility he was so resentful about but felt he couldn't avoid?

When he opened his eyes again, it was getting dark in his room, which meant it was going on five. He jumped up, his heart pounding. Were Thomas and Jeremy back? Where was Palma?

He threw open his bedroom door and looked down the hall. The house seemed empty and quiet. Of course, it was always quiet unless somebody had left water running somewhere or the clock alarm on for hours because they couldn't hear them. But if there was anyone around, there should be some human sounds. He ran downstairs, where it was as still as it had been upstairs. Through the window over the sink, he could see that the lights were on out in Palma's studio. Who did she think was holding things together in here while she was paying attention only to herself?

He picked up the phone and dialed Ivy's. Dr. Roper answered the TTY.

Hi, Theo, he typed. **We were just about to call you. Thomas and Jeremy are staying for dinner. Would you and your mother like to join us?**

Theo exhaled so strongly he could have launched a sailing ship. **Oh, thanks. But I think I'll let the boys have their own night out.**

All right. Probably be good for you and your mom to have a little time together, anyway. The last few weeks must have been hard on you all.

No kidding, Theo thought before he hung up.

As for wanting a little time together, forget it.

He made himself a couple of sandwiches, while he wondered what Ivy was fixing for dinner. He took the sandwiches, balanced on a paper towel, up to his room, where he ate and did his homework. He heard Palma come in from the studio, but he didn't go downstairs. He'd left her a note on the kitchen table about where Jeremy and Thomas were. Let her fend for herself for dinner. The servant was taking the night off.

Later, he heard Jeremy and Thomas come in, stamping and breathing hard from the cold. Another problem with having a deaf family was that Theo couldn't eavesdrop on their conversations. He had to be where he could see them signing to know what was going on.

He went to the head of the stairs and watched them take off their coats. Jeremy spotted him and waved.

Have a good time?

Great, Jeremy signed. **We started a new plane. A bright red Lockheed Vega like the one Amelia Earhart flew solo across the Atlantic. And Ivy made a great dinner. You should have come.**

Well. I had a lot to do. I'll come down and help Pop upstairs and get him ready for bed.

Thomas held up his hand. **I'll get myself upstairs. If I can walk all the way to Ben's, I can get up a few steps by myself.**

Okay. But he stood, watching anxiously as Thomas slowly came up, and Jeremy with him, playfully pushing from behind. Thomas hung on to the banister with his strong hand and took his time, making sure his weaker leg cleared the steps. It took him a while, but he made it, with a pleased expression on his face.

No problem, he signed. **And I can get myself ready for bed, too, so you guys go do your own stuff. Your old man's on the way up, so, Theo, you can quit looking so worried.**

Okay, Theo said, still worried.

18

The next morning, Palma was in the kitchen when Theo came down. That was unusual enough, but, even odder, she'd fixed him breakfast. He couldn't remember the last time that had happened. It was a nice breakfast, too—grapefruit and French toast. His own words to Ivy about the significance of feeding people—especially when you didn't have to—echoed in his head. He wished the echoes of suspicion weren't there as well.

Thanks, he signed.

It was fun. It's nice to spend a little quiet time with my big boy.

While he ate, she chatted on to him about how she was going to decorate the house for Christmas, about something funny she'd read in the paper, about something she wanted to do with the garden next spring. She was as animated and charming as only she could be, and he could feel the pull of her full attention, which was so hard to come by, and so radiant and irresistible when it was turned completely your way.

He finished eating, wiped his mouth, and stood. He hated to be the one to break the spell, but he was going to go to school, and he wanted to be sure she knew that. **Got to go, Palma.**

She stood, too, and her expression changed. **Where are you going?**

To school. He grabbed his backpack.

But I thought you were going to stay—

I'm going to school. Harry and Hazel will be by soon to hang out with Pop.

I told you to make them stop coming. Her elegant signing was as expressive as a voice could have been. He definitely heard the imperious tone.

If you want them to stop coming, you tell them. But you'd better ask Pop first if that's okay with him. And he left.

Concentration at school was impossible, of course. Would Palma really kick Harry and Hazel out? What would happen to Thomas if she did? What kind of a mess would he find when he got home?

He looked for Ivy and saw her through crowds of other people three different times. And each time their eyes met, Ivy looked away. Once she completely turned her back on him. He'd have had to be a moron not to get the message. Especially since she was with Mr. Tennis the time she turned her back on him.

He caught the late bus, postponing going home as long as he could, and although Ivy was on it, too, she passed him without a glance and sat in the very last seat.

He walked from the bus stop as slowly as possible, and got even slower as he went up the front walk. He cracked open the front door and listened.

The first thing he heard was Hazel's crazy laugh. He shut the door and she called out, "Is that you, Theo?"

"The one and only." He went into the living room, where Jeremy sat at a table by the fire with Hazel, working a jigsaw puzzle. At an adjoining table sat Thomas and Harry working on one, too.

"We had to separate them," Hazel said. "They kept butting in on our puzzle. How was your day?"

"How was *yours*?"

She gave him a mystified look. "Well, fine. The usual. Why?"

"You didn't see Palma?"

"No. Generally she's here for a minute or two before she goes to the studio, but this morning I guess she'd already started working."

"Oh." What was he to make of this? Was she still waiting for him to do the dirty work of firing Harry and Hazel? Well, she could wait forever for that one.

Hazel signed to Jeremy, **Don't let your dad touch this puzzle. You and I can work on it again tomorrow. Or maybe you can get it finished before I come in the morning.**

Okay, Jeremy signed.

Hazel tapped Thomas on the shoulder and, when she had his attention, signed, **We'll see you tomorrow. Keep your paws off my puzzle.**

Even after they'd gone, Jeremy and Thomas still leaned over their puzzles. Theo thought about what a difference Harry and Hazel had made for Thomas in the short time they'd been coming. They'd taken him for long walks, played cards and done puzzles with him to sharpen his mind and his manual skills, and, best of all, treated him like a regular person, not a patient. How dare Palma disregard that, and worse, disrespect how valuable they'd been.

He could only hope that Thomas would give her a fight if she tried to get them to leave, but he wasn't sure. Thomas, along with everyone else, had been awfully good at letting Palma have her own way for way too long.

He went upstairs and took his college applications out of the trash. Family first, okay, but maybe Penn or Drexel would fit into the new situation after all, even if they didn't have a linear accelerator and a plasma fusion lab the way MIT did.

. . .

Later he asked Thomas, **What about going back to work? I know you've been talking to your boss about it.**

I'll start going in a couple of hours a day at the beginning of December. Harry's been helping me with my tools, and I can use most of them if I just take my time. My hand should be much stronger in three weeks, especially with Harry helping me with my exercises.

You know you don't have to. There's enough money from Palma's sculptures so you don't have to work, isn't there?

I want to work. Thomas's hand movements were emphatic. **I like to work. I'll go nuts sitting home all day. Especially without Harry and Hazel for company.**

Without Harry and Hazel? Theo asked.

Well, they can't hang around here forever. They've got lives.

I think you're part of their lives now.

That's good. And they'll always be part of mine. But I don't need a baby-sitter all the time anymore. Really, Theo, I'm much better. He took a long look at Theo. **Yeah. I know you were scared. So was I. And we'll probably always be a little scared from now on. But I know nothing stays the same forever. Change is the one thing you can always count on, and you have**

to be able to get used to it. I'm different now, but I'm not an invalid. There's nothing I'd hate more.

The Posse ate without Palma that night, and she wasn't in the kitchen making breakfast for Theo the next morning either. The fact that she was sulking didn't worry Theo. The possibility that she might be planning another way to keep him out of school did.

In study hall he worked on his college applications and looked for Ivy. He made more progress on the applications.

He still hadn't spoken to Ivy by the time Thomas went back to work three weeks later. She continued to bring dinner four times a week, but by some magic, it was always left in the refrigerator without his ever seeing her do it.

He saw her often, of course, at school in the last days before Christmas vacation, but she always kept just far enough away from him that it was impossible for him to say anything to her. Even though she didn't seem to ever actually see him, she apparently had a kind of batlike sonar that kept her from getting too close to him.

He thought he could catch whiffs of cinnamon and cloves in the air in the wake of where she had walked.

Jeremy and Thomas regularly went over to fly the airplanes, and came home with plates of Christmas cookies. Jeremy asked him why he didn't go with them anymore, and Theo had to tell him that he and Ivy had had a fight.

Well, don't make her any madder, Jeremy signed. **I want her to keep bringing dinner.**

Palma thawed as December progressed, but only, as far as Theo could tell, because she needed his services in the preparations for Christmas: phone calls made and errands run. He did what he had to and otherwise kept out of her way.

Harry and Hazel still wanted to come for a couple of hours every afternoon, even during vacation, in spite of the fact that Theo had told them he could handle things alone.

"Oh, go Christmas shopping, or ice-skating, or something," Harry said to Theo. "I want to play cards with your dad."

Harry and Hazel had given him the best possible Christmas present—he would have regular free time on his hands, and the sense that everything would be under control at home without his having to do it. It was a strange, even an empty feeling and one, he discovered, that was not entirely welcome.

He thought for the first time in a serious way about what Ivy had said to him: about how he needed to be consumed by his family, that it was part of his identity. He'd dismissed what she said as completely missing the point.

But how was he to account for how useless he felt now, when he would be relieved of so much that he'd felt was burdensome?

. . .

One afternoon a few days before Christmas, he came home from running errands for Palma to find her standing beside Hazel, signing to her while Hazel talked on the phone. Hazel was writing things on a pad. Under what circumstances had Palma and Hazel made this contact? And why was Hazel making Palma's phone calls? That was his job.

Palma motioned Theo in. **Theo.** Her hands danced. **I'm going to have a new show in February. Just a little one for the new pieces I've done since this fall. In spite of everything, I've been able to be productive. I came out of the studio this afternoon all excited because I'd finished some good work and I decided I wanted to show those pieces, and I found darling Hazel here. She called that gallery in San Francisco for me and they agreed to a show and she's helping me with the arrangements. Isn't that wonderful?**

Well, it should have been. Why wasn't it? Why was he suddenly furious with Palma for letting someone else do what he'd once done? And hated doing. And why was she using Hazel, whom she'd so recently wanted him to get rid of?

Hazel put down the phone. "What a nice man," she said to Theo. "He's so excited about your show. He doesn't care if you have only eight pieces." She signed that to Palma at the same time she said it to Theo.

Palma put her arms around Hazel, kissed her cheek, did the same to Theo, and rushed off to tell Thomas.

When she'd gone, Hazel said to Theo, "Well, she's nothing like what Ivy said. She's lovely, isn't she? And what a dynamo."

"Yeah," Theo said.

"She says she wants me to help her arrange the whole thing. Can you imagine? I have no idea how to do it. But she said you'd done it for her before, and if you could do it, so could I."

Was that supposed to be a compliment to Hazel, or an insult to Theo? How clever of Palma to be able to do both at the same time. He knew he should have felt relieved that he didn't have to make all those crazy phone calls this time, but somehow he didn't.

"Well, let's go celebrate with them," Hazel said. Her cheeks were pink and there was a bounce in her step. Theo could already imagine how much mileage she'd get out of informing her bingo group that she was now a famous sculptor's representative.

Palma explained about the show to Thomas. He sat in his chair by the fire watching her. Theo thought he looked tired—but then, he had a right to be. He'd been back at work for a couple of weeks and it hadn't been easy for him. He'd tried too hard, and his performance had disappointed him.

Wonderful, he signed. It was a one-handed sign, and Theo frowned as he noticed how slowly he signed, even with his good hand.

When Hazel and Palma went back to the studio to talk about the new show, Theo asked Thomas, **Are you okay, Pop? You seem tired.**

I am tired. Going back to work's been harder than I thought it would be. But I'm sure I'll get used to it. I just have to build up my strength some more.

Why don't you take a nap? I'll wake you up in time for dinner.

Good idea. Make sure you get me up. You know how I hate to miss one of Ivy's meals. He pushed himself slowly out of his chair and went to the stairs. Theo could see how heavily he was leaning on the banister, and moved to help him. Then he checked himself. Thomas wanted to be independent. He had to allow him to be.

He sat by the Christmas tree and wondered what he would ask Santa for if he believed that Santa could bring him anything he wanted, and if he believed that he'd been nice enough not to get a stocking full of coal. He'd probably been more naughty than nice this year, but never mind. He made his list anyway.

1. Ivy speaking to him again
2. Admission to MIT
3. Thomas completely recovered

Would he wish for his family to hear? he wondered. He couldn't imagine them any way other than how they were.

Would Palma still have been a great sculptor without the inspiration of her deafness? Would Thomas have had the pleasure of his magic and his carpentry?

Jeremy.

He would give Jeremy hearing. That he would do. His brother's life would be easier, there was no question about it. And then Theo wouldn't have to worry about him as he grew up, wouldn't have to feel he always needed to be looking out for him. Or was that something all siblings did? Was he once again mixing up what was connected to deafness and what wasn't?

Such heavy thinking made him drowsy. That and the warmth from the fire sent him gently into sleep.

He woke with a start, thinking he'd heard a sound, but realizing that what had really waked him was the deep silence in the house. Thomas was still napping. Hazel and Palma must still be in the studio, and Harry had taken Jeremy Christmas shopping. He shivered.

He stood, rubbing his hands over his face. Tonight he needed some noise, something for his own ears to play with. He switched on the tinny little radio in the kitchen, bought by Thomas as a surprise for Theo when he was nine. At the time Theo had been disappointed at its poor quality, but now he understood more. How was Thomas to judge the fidelity of a radio? One thing he couldn't forget was Jeremy, resting his hand on the radio, feeling its vibrations and its warmth, asking him if words were warm.

He looked out the window over the sink, across the dark yard to where squares of light from the studio fell on the brown lawn. What the heck were they doing out there?

He turned on the oven and took Ivy's dinner out of the refrigerator. He stood holding the aluminum containers, imagining Ivy's hands under his. All he actually had was her fingerprints and that wasn't good enough. He shook his head and stuck the dinner containers in the oven. Harry and Jeremy knew what time dinner was. If they weren't home by then, they'd probably stopped for a burger. He'd set the table and then go wake Thomas, give him a chance to come to while he went out and got Hazel and Palma.

In the bedroom, Theo saw that Thomas was taking himself a serious nap—one that involved removing his shoes and slacks and getting under the covers, not just lying down on the spread. He must have been more tired than Theo had realized.

He wished he could wake Thomas gradually by banging around the room a little, the way he would have if his dad could hear. Being awakened by a touch was always so startling and could even be frightening.

He sighed and touched his father on the shoulder. Thomas didn't move.

Poor guy, Theo thought. Maybe I should just let him sleep. He's been working awfully hard at his therapy, and going back to work has been a strain, too. But then he remembered how Thomas had insisted on being awakened for dinner, so he shook him harder.

Still he slept.

"Hey, Pop," Theo said automatically, even knowing Thomas couldn't hear him, as he shook him again. Then he touched his hand—the hand that had made their furniture and done magic tricks for them and told corny jokes—and found it cold. And he knew.

He went to his room and put all his completed college applications into his wastebasket once again, and then went downstairs to tell Palma.

19

Hazel and Harry made all the arrangements for the funeral. Given their ages, they'd had plenty of experience at it. Palma was hysterical, either weeping uncontrollably or so sedated that she slept for hours. Theo was numb, and Jeremy was bewildered.

But he was getting so much better, Jeremy kept signing, as if Thomas's death was a mistake that could be reversed if only he could explain it to the right person.

Thomas was buried two days before Christmas. It was cold with rain that fell heavy and thick, almost but not quite sleet. It seemed to be dark by three-thirty.

A surprising number of people came to the service—and not just people from the Deaf Club. Thomas's work colleagues were there, and people from the Society of Magicians, some of Theo's classmates and their families, admirers of Palma's art, and friends of Harry's and Hazel's.

Ivy was at the graveside, hunched inside a long black coat, the purple streak in her hair a bright contrast to the bleakness of the place and the occasion.

Theo wanted to talk to her, but it was impossible. He was completely occupied with Palma, interpreting the service and all but holding her up. He had no room for his own grief or his own concerns.

Hazel had arranged for Ivy to do the food afterward, when everyone came back to the house, but she'd stayed mostly in the kitchen, unobtrusively dishing things up and washing used plates.

By the time the crowd had cleared out and Palma had gone upstairs for another of her drugged sleeps, Ivy had cleaned up and left without ever speaking to him. But in the middle of the kitchen table was an envelope with his name on it.

Inside was a single piece of paper with the words I'M SO SORRY. IVY.

He closed his eyes and put the note back inside the envelope. Of course, she meant she was sorry about Thomas. But did she also mean she was sorry about their argument? What was the etiquette with arguments anyway? Who was supposed to apologize? The one who started the argument, or the other one? And who *had* started their argument? He couldn't even remember how it had happened—only something about geese, and that they'd said unkind things to each other.

Or maybe he'd been the one to say unkind things. Maybe she'd only said things that were true.

It didn't matter anymore what she'd said, even if it had all been true. He was lost inside a sorrow so big it made everything else seem irrelevant. Anyway, there was no argument she could possibly provide now that would make it reasonable for him to leave for college. Even forgetting how desperate Palma was, how could he go off and leave Jeremy with no one? Even if he'd been able to imagine going away to college while Thomas was still alive—and he hadn't really been able to—he certainly couldn't now. It simply no longer calculated.

Ivy would have liked that: mathematics talk.

He went upstairs to get Jeremy settled and then to go to bed himself, though sleep wasn't something he actually did much of. He was the opposite of zonked-out Palma: he lay awake with dry eyes and numb heart, thinking about Thomas, about the hole his absence made in his, Theo's, life and in his heart. It was simply unbelievable that he was gone forever.

Forever.

There was no way for him to compute how long that was.

He turned his mind away from it, thinking instead about the applications in his unemptied trash cans, most of which had had a due date of January first.

. . .

In the morning, he realized with a shock of disbelief that it was Christmas Eve. How could normal things continue to happen when it didn't seem that anything was normal with him? He wondered if Christmas would ever again have any magic, or if it would become only a milestone commemorating another anniversary of his father's death.

Jeremy was sitting in the kitchen over an untouched bowl of cereal. **Where do you think Dad is?** he signed.

Theo took a deep breath and replied, **Somewhere where he's doing magic tricks and flying airplanes, and making beautiful furniture. And keeping an eye on us.**

You really think so?

Yes. He didn't know if he really believed that, but he wanted to. And he knew Jeremy wanted to, too.

Can he hear?

If he wants to.

Okay. And Jeremy raised a spoonful of cereal to his mouth. He put his spoon down. **I don't think we should have Christmas this year.**

I don't either, Theo told him. **Maybe next year.**

I got Pop a good present, too. A new magic trick. What am I going to do with it?

Theo thought about how hard it had been for Thomas to admit that he could no longer do the tricks he'd loved to astound them with. **Maybe you could learn to do it. Pop would like that.**

Jeremy nodded and began eating.

Palma came downstairs about noon. By then Hazel was there in the kitchen making soup. Harry had taken Jeremy ice-skating. Palma stood in the kitchen doorway in a wrinkled bathrobe, her hair stiff and messy, her eyes swollen.

"Here," Hazel said, handing Theo the spoon. "You stir this." **Let's go have a bath**, she signed to Palma. Like a zombie, Palma turned and let Hazel take her back upstairs.

Theo was standing at the stove stirring the soup when he heard a tap at the back door. Through the glass he could see Ivy bundled against the cold, her mittened hands holding a basket. He turned down the heat under the soup and let her in.

"Hi." A wedge of cold followed her through the door.

"Hi," she said, not meeting his eyes as she shut the door. "It looks like snow." She held the basket out to him. "I brought food. It's all I could think of to do."

How could he ever have been critical of her wish to feed people? Did it really make any difference why she did it? So what if she was compensating for an absent, unnurturing mother? It was still the friendliest, the most comforting, the most welcome thing he could think of. A basket of food spoke more volumes about affection and caring, sorrow and sympathy, hope and forgiveness than either of them could ever have said aloud.

He took the basket. "Thanks. I'm sure it's great, no matter what it is."

She shrugged, still bundled for the cold in the warm kitchen.

"Take off your coat. Can you stay awhile?"

"If it's okay. If you want me to." She made no effort to unbutton her coat or take off her mittens.

"Yeah. I want you to."

With that, she stuffed her mittens in her pockets and shrugged off her coat. She put it over the back of a kitchen chair and stood awkwardly, avoiding his eyes. "What kind of soup are you making?"

"I don't know. Hazel's making it."

"Uh-oh. Why do you think she had me cooking for her?"

"Then let's hope she's just warming up something you made." He gestured to a chair. "Sit down. Please."

Gingerly, Ivy sat on the edge of her chair.

"Speaking of warming up," Theo said, "I've missed you."

"Yeah?" She was wary, but she finally looked directly at him.

"I . . . shouldn't have said what I did. I'm sorry if I hurt you."

"Well, what you said did hurt," she said, fiddling with the salt and pepper shakers, "but you weren't wrong."

"I don't care about that. Who cares why you cook? I'm just glad you do."

She watched the salt and pepper shakers intently. "Some

things you never get over. That's the truth. I'll always miss her, even when I can't remember her."

Without either of them saying it, they both knew that Theo would always miss Thomas, too. And that Theo's life would change now in ways he couldn't predict because of his father's absence.

"I know," he finally said. He sat down across from her. "It's weird, but I still can't feel very much. I can't believe what's happened. I keep thinking I'll wake up and my old life will be back."

"I'm not sure you'll ever get used to it. I hate that word *closure*. There's no such thing. I still dream I have a mother."

"Maybe that's how you do still have one." He didn't mention that her dream mother was probably a better one than her real one.

"It's how you can still have your dad, too."

But that wasn't how Theo wanted his dad. He wanted the real thing.

She sighed and said, "I know," as if she'd read his mind. "Remember that day we talked about zoos? When we wondered if the animals saved from extinction might have preferred it if they'd known the cure was being kept caged up?"

"Yeah." How did she keep tuning to the same frequency he was on?

"Well, maybe your dad would have felt that way if he knew he'd never be able to work or do magic or be strong again."

"So now he's extinct but he doesn't mind?"

She lifted one shoulder and gave him a melancholy half-smile. "It's a thought."

He couldn't help remembering the day Thomas had told him how much he'd hate to be an invalid. For him, that would have been like being in a cage.

Absently, Theo unpacked the basket. There was a coffee cake and some pears and several wedges of different cheeses.

"When I'm upset," she said, "all I want to eat is fruit and bready things."

He sliced the coffee cake and gave her a plate. Then he made one for himself. He tasted and said, "It's good. Very therapeutic."

"I wish it was the cure. But I don't think there is one."

Hazel came in then, holding Palma by the hand. Palma had on a fresh robe and her hair was wet, but combed.

Ivy stood and said, **Hello**, but Palma looked at her as if she didn't see her. Hazel maneuvered Palma into a chair, and Ivy pushed her untouched slice of coffee cake across the table to her.

Palma shook her head, but Ivy signed, **Just try it. You have to eat.**

Theo thought there was even a maternal tone to her signing.

Obediently, Palma picked up the fork and took a bite. She chewed and took another, then settled down to finishing the slice.

"Thanks, Hazel," Theo said.

Hazel put her hand on his shoulder. "It's nothing. I like doing it, though I certainly wish the circumstances were different. I was awful fond of your dad." She paused when her eyes filled with tears, and waited until they subsided. "It's good to be needed again. You can't know how good because you've never not been needed."

"Well—thanks all the same. I couldn't do for Palma what you've done."

"No," Hazel said quietly. "You couldn't. Don't forget, I've been widowed, too."

He had forgotten. All he'd thought about Hazel was how much fun she was, how lively, how engaged in life. Had she once been as catatonic as Palma was now? Could Palma someday have her life back? A life with a different shape, to be sure, but one that was full and good?

He didn't know what the secret was to making that happen.

While Palma finished her coffee cake, Hazel poured the soup into a plastic container and washed out the pot. "When that's cool, you put it in the freezer for later, Theo, you hear me?" Hazel said, her back to Theo while she worked at the sink.

Palma was bent over her coffee cake as Ivy quickly signed to Theo, **The disposal's going to enjoy that more than you are, if you're smart.**

Theo surprised himself with a laugh that popped unexpectedly from his throat. He'd never expected to laugh again.

"What?" Hazel said, turning her head, her hands still in the dishwater.

"Nothing," Theo said. "Just something caught in my throat."

It came to him that even though Hazel was a lousy cook, she was doing the same thing Ivy, with much tastier results, did. She was caring. What she'd made them was a pot of love. He didn't like to think of pouring it away—though he didn't actually like to think of eating it, either.

"Well, you be careful," she said, going back to her chore. "We don't need any more calamities around here."

"I'm going to walk Ivy home," Theo said to Ivy's surprised face. "I'll be back later."

"You go ahead. It's good for you to get out."

Outside in the cold dry air, heavy with the threat of snow, Theo felt his head expand. Hazel was right—he'd been inside for too long. Life was still happening, whether or not he thought it was possible.

"It's odd to see all the Christmas decorations," he told Ivy. "We canceled Christmas this year."

"Good. A year from now you'll be feeling a lot different. You can decide then what to do about it. When you're home from college."

"Get serious, Ivy. You know I can't go anywhere. It was bad enough when I thought I'd have to stay here to see to Pop, but now—well, now it's even worse."

"It's the same." He could see her stubborn chin set itself.

"Look. I don't want to fight again. But you must know it really is different now."

"How? Your mother still needs fussing over. Your household still needs organizing. Jeremy still needs company and guidance. Those are your life facts. Everybody's got them, and you just have to accept yours. What's *really* different?"

If she couldn't see it, well, he couldn't explain it to her. "Anyway, what do you care if I go to college or not?"

She turned on him, her eyes full of tears, her cheeks flushed with cold and emotion. "Because you're somebody who *should* go. You're not like those lunks who just want to go for the beer parties and the girls. You've got a brain and a heart and you'll appreciate it—and probably learn how to do something really useful, like build a peace machine or environment-friendly cars or something."

"A peace machine?" he asked, bemused by how her mind worked even as she was driving him nuts.

"Oh, I don't know," she said, swiping her mittened hand across her eyes. "But it's a good idea, don't you think?"

"Yeah, it's a good idea." His heart felt as if a friendly hand had given it a little squeeze. He *would* appreciate college—probably the same way Thomas had appreciated Gallaudet—not only because he'd never been one hundred percent sure that he'd get there but because he really did want to immerse himself in all the new things there were for him to learn; things he knew he hadn't even heard of yet, but that might be just what would change the direction of his life.

Just as Thomas's death had, he reminded himself, coming back to earth with a thump.

"Do it," Ivy urged. "Just send in your applications. You've written them, I know you have. Your mother'll sign the application fee checks if you put them in front of her. She won't even ask what they're for."

"You're saying I should trick her?"

"No. I'm saying you should let her help you get what you need, even when she's too lost to think of it herself. Then at least you'll have options for next fall. If you don't apply anywhere, the door is closed for next fall—and if another year has to go by, you'll be even deeper in the quicksand."

Quicksand. He hadn't thought of it like that, but that's how it felt.

When he didn't respond, she said, "Well, just think about it."

They'd reached her house. "You want to come in?" she asked.

"No, thanks. I want to stay outside for a while. I feel more . . . more normal somehow, out here."

"Will you . . . will I hear from you?"

"I wouldn't be surprised," he said, and went off down the sidewalk, not looking back. He didn't want to look behind himself at anything.

Almost two blocks from Ivy's, it started to snow. The flakes were small and dry at first, and slid easily off the nylon of his jacket. But they began to come faster and wetter, to stick more on the ground and on cars and bushes and his jacket. If he just stood still and did nothing, he understood, he would soon be completely buried.

At home, Palma, still in her bathrobe, was asleep on the couch, while Hazel sat in the rocker watching TV and knitting something. Harry and Jeremy worked a jigsaw puzzle by the fire. Theo recognized it as the same one Thomas and Harry had been doing such a short time ago. The scene would have looked like a family if only Theo hadn't known who was missing.

"You okay?" Hazel asked Theo after he'd hung up his jacket.

"Yeah," he said. "I think so."

He went upstairs and stood looking out the window. Darkness was settling among the bushes in the garden as they fast disappeared under the snow. Soon, he knew, the garden would be full of nothing but smooth white lumps. If those bushes could stand up and shake themselves free, they could look like what they were. But as long as they couldn't move, couldn't do anything to help themselves, they would just be covered up. Helpless and muffled and obliterated.

And beautiful in the blue-white dusk light. Beautiful and cold and still as death.

He turned from the window, tears streaming down his cheeks, and retrieved his completed applications from the trash. Then he went to his parents'—now just Palma's—bedroom and took the checkbook from the bureau drawer. He began filling out checks.

20

AUGUST

I don't want to go back-to-school shopping, Jeremy signed. Why can't I just wear my old stuff?

Because it doesn't fit, Theo signed.

And it's raggedy, Palma signed.

And it's faded, Hazel signed.

And it's ugly, Harry signed, making a face. Y-u-c-k, he finger-spelled.

Oh, okay, Jeremy said, with a great, resigned show of sighing. But do you all have to go with me?

No, Theo signed. We don't even want to. Who would you like to be the unlucky one to have to accompany you?

I'd love to help, Palma said, but I've got this deadline, you know.

We know, Theo, Hazel, Harry and Jeremy all signed at the same time.

I want Harry first so we can go fast. Then we'll have lunch with Theo and Hazel. Then Theo can go with me to the magic shop to buy some new tricks. All the old ones of Pop's are too easy now. Then Hazel can go with me to fix up whatever Harry and I did wrong.

They all laughed, and Jeremy went off to get ready.

Theo went up to assess his own wardrobe. He had plenty of money to spend on some new stuff from working as Ivy's assistant in her growing catering business. As he liked to tell her, he was the brawn and she was the brains—and the beauty—of the operation. Her customers were sure going to miss her when she left for Boston to go to culinary school. Her father would miss her, too. But with Jeremy and Harry over there so much working on the airplanes— they were busy with Charles Lindbergh's Ryan NYP *Spirit of St. Louis* prop plane now—he wouldn't be alone too much of the time. And Harry had big plans to get him into model boat building next.

Palma had plenty of money, too. The show of her "grief pieces," as she called them, had sold out, and the critics were saying it was the most emotional, passionate work she'd ever done. The series she was working on now was called *Path of Recovery*—not *Path* to *Recovery*, the way everybody said it should be—since she said she wasn't sure that there was an end to the path.

But it's important to keep walking on it and not sit down for too long, Hazel kept reminding her.

Theo got a little tired of Hazel's admonitions sometimes, but he couldn't really complain about how seriously she took her job as Palma's household organizer. And she was somehow able to bully Palma into behaving herself in a way that Theo would never understand. Maybe what Palma had needed all along was just somebody tough enough to tell her, with no nonsense, to cut out her imperious behavior. Or maybe it had something to do with Thomas and the big hole he'd left behind.

Harry was supposedly Hazel's assistant, but mostly what he liked to do was hang out with Jeremy, and not just at Ben Roper's making models. He'd coached Jeremy's deaf Little League team, and even though they'd won only four games, they'd had a great time and wanted him to coach their soccer team in the fall, since their previous coach had gotten a job transfer and moved away. He said he would if they'd promise to buy him a burger after every game even if they lost. They were thinking about it.

Harry wasn't getting any younger—though he and Hazel both should be on posters advertising how to age—and Theo worried about heart attacks and apoplexy when he watched Harry hollering from the Little League sidelines—he kept forgetting his team couldn't hear him. But for every day that Harry and Hazel wanted to help out the family—to actually be *part* of the family—Theo was grateful beyond measure. Maybe he couldn't change his life facts, as Ivy called them, but he'd learned he could work with them. Family first no longer meant his doing everything by himself. Now he knew how fast things could change—and how hard, yet how necessary, it was to be able to keep making new plans. When Harry and Hazel couldn't, or didn't want to, help anymore, he'd have to find somebody else. He didn't like to think about that, but he knew he could do it.

He inspected a gray sweater with a hole in the elbow and wondered if that would be okay to take to MIT. He sure didn't want to haul it all the way to Boston and wear it some night when Ivy would tell him it shouldn't have made the trip.

Jeremy came into his room while he was holding up the sweater.

Pop used to take me back-to-school shopping, he signed.

Yeah. I know. Theo sat down on his bed, the sweater in his lap. Jeremy sat next to him.

I want him to do it again.

Theo put his arm around Jeremy's shoulders. **Yeah. I know that, too.**

I like Harry. A lot. But he's not Pop.

Nope. Theo couldn't think of any words that would

make them hurt less about Thomas. That was a life fact.

Pop would be glad you have Harry, though.

You're right. He would.

And he'd be glad about the magic you're doing. And the models. And your sports.

Do you think he'd be glad you're going away to school?

I hope so. From now on, we have to guess.

I don't have to like that, do I?

Nope.

Okay. I have to go now. Harry's waiting.

Buy something really cool.

Like you'd know what that was, Jeremy said as he went out the door.

Laughing, Theo folded the sweater and put it back in the drawer. It was going with him. It didn't have to be perfect. It just had to be something he was used to and liked and wanted to keep close to him, even in a new place.